I0647853

The Diary

of a

Caregiver

Gigi

Daly

The Diary of a Caregiver
Publisher: DSA (Daly Strategic Associates, Inc.) Cincinnati, Ohio
Book Website: GoodinGray.com

Library of Congress Cataloging-in-Publication Data:
Daly, Gigi, 1956—author.
Diary Of A Caregiver / Gigi Daly.
          p. cm.
Subjects: 1. Caregiving. 2. Mental health. 3. Self-help.
I. Title. II. Title The Diary of a Caregiver.

Identifiers:
ISBN 978-1-7338327-4-8 (hardcover)
ISBN 978-1-7338327-3-1 (paperback)
1st edition, September 2024
Copyright © 2024 by Geralyn Daly.

DSA

"To the Hardship and Heroship of Caregiving."

Introduction

Everyone will be a Caregiver at some point along the circle of life.

The Diary of a Caregiver is a metafictional novel. Mrs. Patstegre, the main character, entwines the realness of her Caregiving life with her fictional stories of free expression, showing the immense need for change for and toward the mentally ill. Their painful suffering has gone on for too long.

Mrs. Patstegre, creator and narrator, in *The Diary of a Caregiver*, reveals her personal diary entries filled with opinions, tips, experiences, and coping skills to help Caregivers and the people she cares for persevere.

Mrs. Patstegre's Caregiving world rotates around her son Speet, her dear friend Clippy, her sister Effie, the homeless, the elderly who she calls her Lovelies, and others that she cares for. Watching some of these loved ones suffer from torturing, uncontrollable symptoms, decades of stigmatic slurs, and unjust remarks surrounding mental illness, makes her anger burst.

Her anguish causes her to develop a form of lucid dreaming she calls mind killing. Her creative mind killing dreams scream for justice and prowl for prey consisting of stigma spitters, fentanyl killers, and other tormentors. These anger releasing dreams are confused meaning to the naked flesh, dot-to-dot connection to the ones who have been skinned. Please *bare* that in mind when you think her fictional mind killing dreams are too extreme.

Deep emersion with Mrs. Patstegre's expressive diary will spark your compassion for caring for others. If you are a Caregiver or a future Caregiver, Mrs. Patstegre's unique voice will help you deal with loneliness, unfairness, anger, and persecution. She will show the importance of communication and the necessity for self-care.

The Diary of a Caregiver melts edges of traditional definitions of words and ignites new meanings. Nouns become verbs and verbs become nouns. Mrs. Patstegre twists her words and creates merry-go-round phrases to show how daily life can go from silence to ear piercing frequencies.

There are a few other things to be mindful of while reading *The Diary of a Caregiver*.

- o Inanimate objects come to life to illustrate the solitary existence of Mrs. Patstegre.
- o Caregiver and other nouns she believes are deserving of respect are capitalized.
- o Her diary covers several years.

Diary Entry 1 - December 13. End of Year One.

"Good morning, Mrs. Patstegre."

"Good morning, Crystal. You look picture perfect. I'm lucky if I get up and get my jeans on, let alone curl my hair and even think about putting on a skirt like the one you have on," I said.

"Thanks, Mrs. Patstegre. I would love to wear my jeans like you to Concerned Care but as we both know, part of volunteering as the receptionist includes wearing a skirt or a dress," Crystal said.

"Yes, I know," I said.

"Hey, Mrs. Patstegre, it's Friday. Do you have plans for the weekend?" Crystal asked.

I thought about saying that I might mind kill - a term I used to kill in a dream. Crystal was sweet. She, of course, would think I was kidding.

"No plans. I'm going to watch a movie. It's supposed to snow on and off for the next couple of weeks. Fort Lace, our wonderful Midwest town, might even have a white Christmas," I answered.

Crystal smiled. I smiled back.

"Crystal, I will see you later. I'm off to put my gray, scalloped apron on and put together my Care-Cart," I said.

Crystal encouraged me to go out. I had developed a significant social handicap since Mr. Patstegre died ten years ago. It was Speet, my son, a few close family members, my best friend Clippy, my work contacts, and Caregiving skills that vined and veined my life with continued growth.

I enjoyed my volunteer position at Concerned Care Nursing Home. I was called the Care-Cart Lady. I used a gray cart to carry out my job. I rolled the cart into the residents' rooms offering various newspapers, magazines, pens and paper, seasonal gifts, and the like. I talked with each resident if they wanted to. I listened and paid attention to them, all things they deserved from their families.

Today I was concentrating on a new resident, Ms. File. I was told she never married, used to be a high school history teacher, and did not have family visitors.

"Knock, knock, Ms. File. I am the Care-Cart Lady. May I come in?" I asked.

"Yes, please do. I've heard about you," Ms. File answered.

I walked into Ms. File's room. All the rooms on her floor had a bedroom, a small sitting room, a tiny kitchen, and a good size bathroom.

"I am Mrs. Patstegre, (pronounced Pats – Sta – Gree). It's nice to meet you, Ms. File. I volunteer as much as I can. This in-care nursing unit that you live in along with twenty or so other lovely people is where I volunteer my time. My Care-Cart has magazines, newspapers, medically approved snacks from the nursing staff, paper, pencils, pens, various knick-knacks, and seasonal gifts," I said.

"How wonderful. I will take *The Wall Street Journal* if you have it on your cart," Ms. File said.

"I do have *The Wall Street Journal*, Ms. File. Here you go. I noticed artwork, signed by you, on your walls. How long have you been painting?" I asked.

"I started when I retired at sixty-five and have been painting ever since. At seventy-five my health got the best of me. I never married and did not have children. Concerned Care Nursing Home seemed the best option to call my new home. I am lucky to be able to continue my painting here," Ms. File answered.

"I am glad you are here at Concerned Care, Ms. File," I said.

I said good-bye to this white-haired, medium build woman. She wore all black. I related to that. Her funky rimmed glasses, full of four different colors, yellow, pink, brown, and blue, made you happy just looking at her. I believed Ms. File would become one of my favorites at Concerned Care.

I finished my rounds with care.

Diary Entry 2 - December 14

How did one explain pain that made your whole-body ache? How did one explain the nauseating feeling that never left?

I explained it with mind killing dreams. My mind connected to a wavelength of pain. Someone I loved was taken. Disgust rose out of my pain, love, care, and fury. Dignity came from mind killings with displays of disgust. Disgusting Dignity was necessary for me to live.

Diary Entry 3 - December 15

I swam beneath water most of the day searching for everything and searching for nothing, trying to get to the other side. I swam slow syncopated strokes. I never surfaced to take a breath the whole time under water. I did not need to. Part of me had died. Breathing would never be the same.

Diary Entry 4 - January 6. Year Two.

It was a cold morning. Christmas came and went.

I held up my arms, eyes closed, and said, "I, Mrs. Patstegre, need to release my anger. My love equals my angry hate."

I opened my eyes. Did I see the ceiling shake a little? No, I couldn't have.

I had a cleaning job today. I started cleaning five years ago for short term gratification and exercise, not for consistency. Most who hired me knew that I deep cleaned for them once and only with a rare likeness to the family, did I come back for a second cleaning. I focused on the clean, not the un-clean pain of loss.

"I drive hard. I drive fast. I drive humor. My skeleton is my skin, and my skin is my skeleton. Bones are tough. They withstand the heat of my bitterness and the cold of the world," I said out loud.

My alarm went off. I kicked the blankets off. I pulled myself into my white tiled shower with a matching fish border. White tile was not a problem for me to keep clean. I was a squeegee cleaner. After a hot shower, which lowered stress from my muscles and mind, I squeegeed the tile walls spotless. The satisfaction strokes on the tile injected tinges of joy beneath the hardness within me.

With wet hair, I pulled holey blue jeans on and a black t-shirt from my mid twentieth century, maple wood dresser. Matching pieces of furniture lined the walls of my bedroom.

The solidness of the wood floor led me to my beat-up, multi-colored tennis shoes in my closet. The clothes in the closet looked sad. They remained on their hangars of confinement with little to no touching from their owner, me.

This weight bearing person frightened me every time I was in front of a mirror. "Is that really you, Mrs. Patstegre?" I asked as I looked at myself. That is not how I wanted to look. This extra, I do not know how many pounds over where I should be, was stigma-based.

The hangars, with vivid colors of clothes on them, became visions of faces of hope as my hand entered the closet.

"Pick me, pick me. I want some sunshine on me. I want to give you comfort. You wear the same black this, and the same black that, every day," hangar face after hangar face said.

"Sush, I will wear you all someday when I can," I said.

I grabbed my over-sized blue jean jacket and off I went.

I ran down twelve oak stairs, locked up, and sped ten miles to my cleaning job.

I parked Bessie, the name I gave my trusted and loyal car, in the driveway of my cleaning job. Bessie was a four-wheel drive, V8, cream colored, hell of a car. I was determined to make it to at least 300,000 miles with her.

I grabbed my cleaning products, Vacky, Shiffty, and Minnet. Vacky was my four-foot super sucking machine that vacuumed houses. Shiffty was my feisty, fast broom duster. Minnet was my superb spray making everything shine. Vacky, Shiffty, and Minnet were my friends, tangible gifts of make believe. In other words, Vacky, Shiffty, and Minnet were spars of imagination that would fly into action and dialogue for fun and creative cleaning. My cleaning jobs were real. Vacky, Shiffty, and Minnet were not.

I knocked at the door. The dad of the house, Big Don, answered and stared. There's that look. You know, the how can you clean for a living look. I've seen it before. If only they knew what that look could cost them.

"Come on in, Mrs. Patstegre. It is nice to meet you. We will be gone most of the day so you will have the house to yourself to clean," Big Don said.

Big Don, his wife, Ciathara, little Don, and his brother Ted headed toward the door. My hind legs mindfully kicked them as they walked out.

"Bye, bye," I said.

Their house was not too big. I was sure we could finish cleaning before they got home, especially with the help of my imaginary friends, Vacky, Shiffty, and Minnet.

Minnet sprayed herself over the first-floor bathroom. I wiped the walls, the tile, and the sink. Mold and urine were the drink offered during this morning happy hour. Big Don had urine all over the white toilet bowl. Hell, sometimes when the light hit the rim of the bowl, I swear the urine drops connected and spelled asshole. I found anger in everything.

I accidently hit the cinnamon swirl handle and the fart-infested water splashed and hit my face.

"Damn it!" I said.

I ran upstairs to the bedrooms, two steps at a time. I jumped on all the beds. Nothing bad about that. It was good exercise. Then I grabbed three toothbrushes and juggled them.

As I juggled the toothbrushes, I heard a high-pitched noise. I looked up. I noticed that a hamster was staring at me, standing on his hind legs, his claws clutching the cage, and salivating.

"You creepy little thing. You startled me," I said.

I returned the toothbrushes trying to remember where they went and whose was whose.

I asked my eight-ball intuition whether it was the right time to relieve my rage.

"I want to juggle creepy hammy from hand to hand, dizzy him up, and hmmmmmmm, throw him up in the air and put him back in the cage. Should I, do it?" I asked.

"Yes, most definitely," my eight-ball intuition answered.

What was wrong with me? What was making me think bad thoughts?

Watching a loved one suffer loss was the answer.

Disgusting thoughts brought dignity to my release.

I sat down on a pink flowered sofa in Don and Ciathara's bedroom.

I put my hands over my face. I shook a little. How could I have these trance-like thoughts and think hateful actions? I could never hurt an animal.

"Wait, I mean most definitely not," I shouted out in the room.

"Oh, my fickle eight-ball intuition! You are no help today," I said.

We finished cleaning the rest of the house.

I front jumped, legs spreading into a V, parallel with the ground. I thought of memories of my younger cheerleading days, when my hands were innocent, and my jumps were exciting to watch.

I didn't know what east, west, north, or south hands of the compass I was. I had grizzle in my heart, and it wasn't from a heart attack. I was a remnant of the medieval rack that tore my arms and legs out of their sockets. I had to push all my limbs back in to go on.

I walked down the stairs, tired and headachy.

My cleaning friends, Vacky, Shiffty, and Minnet and I made our way to Bessie, my trusted car. I drove home.

Focused care paved the road over the past years. Now disgusting thoughts and actions existed side-by-side with focused care in my mind.

Shoot and splatter, stab and stomp, and punch and twirl thoughts haunted me.

I was confused. Were those disgusting thoughts always there? I knew deep inside they were. They wanted to be free, to be known, if only in my mind.

One thing was for sure. I would never hurt animals in any of my thoughts or actions.

Diary Entry 5 - March 9

Another day without Mr. Patstegre. Our son, Speet, was twenty-four when Mr. Patstegre died. Speet sprouted thirty-four today.

Speet had cherry wood colored hair. It was shoulder length, worn in a man bun most of the time, and framed a sunless face. His dark chocolate eyes and long, black eyelashes appealed to everyone. A scar on his chin line reminded me of days when his tears came from falling.

Now his tears were from trauma endured a couple of years before Mr. Patstegre died.

Speet was taken against his will thirteen years ago at the impressionable age of twenty-one. He was drugged, beaten, robbed, and abused. Drugs, given to him without his knowledge, brainwashed him and put him in a subservient state.

A horrible and morally wrong man kidnapped and hurt our son. Physical descriptions of this evil man were never worth noting. No one wanted his despicable features embedded in their minds.

We used people underground, and on the ground, to find Speet.

Three months of excruciating days and nights had torches of hope and nightmares of death. Silence was this evil man's torture to Mr. Patstegre and me. Visions of mental and physical abuse vomited paths of focus to find Speet at any cost. Mr. Patstegre and I lived with the possibility of never seeing Speet again. No one deserved that kind of fate. No one.

After three months of detectives, forensic psychologists, and retirement money spent to find Speet, he escaped. Our fate had turned. Happiness and care from his return also begot restlessness. Many years later, restless anger begot a diary of release for me.

Mr. Patstegre and I swam deep and hard to help Speet stay afloat through his recovery. Our help was worth the tiredness, aging in a non-wrinkle way, and anger in a discovery way.

Speet experienced bully-like symptoms of despair, irritability, and anxiety. He wore a new brand of make-up, not in the beauty way, in the neuron way. It was called PTSD – Post-Traumatic Stress Disorder.

Psychiatrists, medications, acupuncture, biofeedback, and therapy, all helped in some fashion, never completing the outfit. We shot Speet heart harpoons and arrows of communication. Communication was a must. Mental illness, without connection, could make a beautiful loved one run. That terrified us.

Anger and hate were my peanut butter and jelly that kept me going in the art of predicting, the art of sensing a threatening wind coming, and the art of swimming against any crisis current.

Speet walked down the stairs and into my coffee daydreams of today.

"Good morning, Speet. How did you sleep last night?"

He walked by me. No answer. I thought, the irritability of PTSD – Post-Traumatic Stress Disorder was intolerable to the one who suffered and *heartbraking* to the Caregiver. I sent my missed heart beats to Speet with imaginary hugs.

I reached for cream in the refrigerator.

"Mom, can you give me space? How many times have I said not to come too close to me? I want to cook some eggs. Do you have to get things out of the refrigerator at this exact moment, the same time I am?" Speet asked.

"No, I will get another cup of coffee and sit at the counter," I answered.

I sat still with my hands glued to my coffee mug. I listened.

I watched Speet scramble his eggs.

Mr. Patstegre and I worked hard when he was alive. We had a successful business. When he passed away there was enough money to allow Speet and me to continue to live in our home. Speet needed safe places in the house. We were lucky to be able to provide them.

"I'm sorry, Mom. Why didn't I take a cab that night? I left my friends at the bar and I decided to walk home. As I walked home, I felt dizzy and very drunk. I knew I hadn't drunk enough to have felt that bad. This asshole that talked to me at the bar must have put something in my beer. I felt someone grab me. He kept me drugged and brainwashed. He had me under his thumb until I escaped," Speet said.

Presently, more than a decade later, Speet, at times, was still a prisoner in his head.

"None of what happened to you is your fault. You always see the best in people. Kindness drives your day. People gravitate to you because you are such a good person. Evil people take advantage of sensitivity like yours," I said.

Speet turned, took the pan of eggs off the stove, and ran into the edge of the island.

"Ouch, shit, that hurt," Speet said.

"It's hard, Mom. I try to dismiss the picture of that evil man embedded in my head. Some days are easier to do that than others," Speet said.

With the pan of eggs still in his hand, he reached for a plate with the other hand. He scooped the eggs onto his plate and set the plate down on the counter.

Speet turned around and looked at me. I knew that look. Sometimes, Speet got lost in his thoughts due to his PTSD. This was one of those times.

Speet grabbed a fork from a drawer. He put the fork on the plate of eggs, picked the plate up, and started walking toward me.

His sock-wrapped feet slid. Speet dropped his plate of scrambled eggs.

As bits of yellow flew in the air, Speet shouted, "Shit, fucking, shit. Why can't I sleep? I am clumsy when I don't sleep."

He grabbed a sponge and swept most of the scattered eggs onto his plate. He threw the sponge, plate, and eggs into the sink.

"I'm going back to bed, I love you, Mom," Speet said.

"I love you, too," I said.

Rageful words came from Speet when triggers of the present turned on a faucet of bad memories from the past. When Speet got triggered from misunderstood words and misconstrued actions said and done from people around him, his anger scold-burned everyone including himself. It wasn't Speet's fault. It was the illness's fault. In Speet's case it was PTSD's fault.

Would symptoms like irritability, panic, fear, and anxiety from PTSD last twenty years, thirty years, forever? No one knew.

I paced in the kitchen. I decided to go upstairs and talk with Speet.

I knocked on his door.

"May I come in, Speet, just for a minute?" I asked.

"Okay, Mom, just for a minute."

I sat in a desk chair near his bed. The room was dark. Did the shades pulled past the ledge form a protective barrier from the reality of the outside world for Speet? It did today.

I scooted my chair closer to him.

"Speet, remember when you got back? You had many bad days and long nights. You told me over the years that those bad days and long nights became more tolerable," I said.

Speet elbowed his pose, raised, and rested his head on the palm of his hand.

"Things are better. I try to be aware of present-day triggers that bring on symptoms like rage, irritability, and anxiety. It's just that I can be triggered so fast. Sometimes, I do not even know it is happening," Speet said.

I responded, "Triggers are control freaks of emotions. At least, that's my opinion. Triggers spark symptoms that are part of PTSD. Ugly words, rageful emotions, you know the drill. When you have symptoms from a bad cold and cough…you can't stop coughing at will, just like it's hard to stop the emotional symptoms of PTSD at will."

Speet looked in my eyes.

"You know I do not mean the things I say when I'm triggered," Speet said.

"I know you don't," I said.

"Mom, thanks for talking."

I got up to leave. I looked back at Speet. His eyes were already closed. There seemed to be a peace train circling his old navy-blue quilt from college that he loved. Maybe Mr. Patstegre engineered the peace train from Heaven. I hoped that was true.

Oh, how I missed Mr. Patstegre, the love of my life.

Diary Entry 6 - March 22

The phone rang.

"Hi, Cha Cha. It's nice to hear your voice," I said.

Cha Cha was a beautiful woman. She had highlighted hair which showed off different shades of blonde and brown. Cha Cha wore it long and free except during the dreaded days or weeks of messy hair depression. Her long oval face and wide eyes spoke anxiety without ever speaking a word.

"It's nice to hear your voice, too, Mrs. Patstegre. I know we haven't met that much in person, but we have spoken many times on the phone since my Mother died. I appreciate you keeping in touch with me. I really do," Cha Cha said.

"I will talk with you anytime you need me," I said.

"Mrs. Patstegre, I was wondering if you could please do me a favor. I told my good friend that I would take some boxes of her things to a storage place this week. I can't drag myself out of bed. I don't know when I would feel up to doing this for my friend. Is there any way you can put these boxes in storage for me?" Cha Cha asked.

"Hold on, Cha Cha. Let me look at my schedule," I answered.

As I reviewed my calendar, I recalled how Mr. Patstegre and I met Cha Cha and her Mother. A year after Speet's trauma, Mr. Patstegre and I went to a support group for parents caring for someone with mental illness. We became friends with an elderly woman in the group. Her name was Mrs. Trody, Cha Cha's Mother.

We kept in touch with Mrs. Trody after the group stopped meeting. About a year ago, Mrs. Trody called me and asked me to join her for lunch. She was very sick. She told me she was not expected to live much longer. Mrs. Trody asked if I would check in on Cha Cha when she passed away. There were no relatives in their life. She died several weeks after we met for lunch.

"I'm back Cha Cha. I can come over tomorrow. Is ten o'clock in the morning good for you?" I asked.

"That will be fine. Thanks so much for doing this for me. I don't know what I would do without you," Cha Cha answered.

I said goodbye to Cha Cha.

Diary Entry 7 - March 23

I drove to Cha Cha's apartment. I picked up ten boxes at ten o'clock in the morning. I drove to Shed's Storage Facility. The building was a giant square of individual units. It was brownish red in color and located off the main road in town. I turned into the parking lot. I went inside the main office.

I walked up to a shy, chiseled faced boy behind the counter and spoke.

"I would like some boxes and a storage unit for a month," I said.

"What size boxes would you like and what size storage unit?" chiseled faced boy asked.

He looked at me with an illuminating stare, the kind of stare that spoke to me. The size of his pupils revealed that drugs were the pencil and paper to his daily routine. His eyes reflected sadness. His name tag spelled Ivan.

"I'll take three small, four medium, and three large boxes. I do not need tape. I will take the smallest unit that would hold the ten boxes that I just bought," I answered.

He looked at me, turned, and calculated the total.

"That will be $32.76 for the boxes and $99.00 for unit number 13070 for a month," Ivan said.

Most of the items I picked up from Cha Cha were in beat-up boxes. I thought it would be nice to transfer the items into strong, new ones.

I opened the large back door of Bessie, my car. I brought the new boxes to the back of her. I thanked Bessie for her Labrador loyalty to me and her protective nature. I repacked the items that Cha Cha's friend gave her. I used my own clear tape that I had in Bessie to seal the new boxes.

I leaned over. The receipt from the boxes fell from my pocket. I picked it up and put it in one of my folders in the front seat. My folders had sparkles and colorful designs on them, creativity that elicited a smile. Did I long for plain folders? No, I really didn't. Sameness and boring were what the world called normal. My life leaned the opposite way.

I started Bessie. I proceeded to a locked gate leading to the storage area. I pushed buttons on a square, black box with a code given to me by Ivan. A black iron gate slid open from right to left. I stepped on the gas pedal and pulled forward.

As I drove to the back of the one-story, no window building, another machine needed my fingers to put a code in. The second set of numbers were pressed. The door opened to a dimly lit parking space for Bessie surrounded by a stone wall. I drove Bessie into the garage opening. I touched a button on a pad on the wall to close the door behind me, leaving Bessie and me to listen to the ghosts of unused and used clothes, items probably never to be used again, and bikes that might never be ridden.

Darkness echoed its importance. I got out of Bessie. Oh, how I wished she had legs instead of tires so she could have walked with me down the lonely corridors in front of me.

Bessie and I were the only ones in this section of the building. A map on the wall showed many hallways and hundreds of storage units.

I turned on Bessie's headlights, illuminating the path for me. The light calmed me enough to stack the boxes on a large cart that I found against a wall. I wheeled it to unit 13070, unlocked it, and stacked the ten boxes inside. I locked everything up.

I ran back to Bessie.

Diary Entry 8 - April 6

There were times when my mind took me to the past.

It was a cool April day, eleven years ago. Speet had been back a few years from his traumatic kidnapping.

Speet said he wanted to go out for a while. He was anxious and preoccupied when he left early in the morning.

Speet found safety in our house, not the outdoors. Speet's emotions and flashbacks from Post-Traumatic Stress Disorder – PTSD caused him to make rash decisions.

Speet had been gone all day. Mr. Patstegre and I were worried. We got a call at seven o'clock at night.

"This is Officer Rable from Coball County. Do you have a son, Speet?"

"Yes. Is he alright? Where is he?" I asked.

"He is fine. We have him for questioning. Thank you," the Officer answered.

He hung up.

Mr. Patstegre did not like what he heard. He immediately called our lawyer who called a private detective to find out where Speet was being held. Our lawyer called back and told us to start driving toward The Coball County Police Station.

We pulled into a parking space outside of a one story, almost windowless building. It was dark in the parking lot. Mr. Patstegre and I wondered if we were in the right place. The private detective told our lawyer where Speet was. We must be in the right place.

We were startled by a comment said by a uniformed man.

"Get out of that parking space. That is my parking space," he said.

Why did some people of authority act like this? Most didn't.

"Okay, we will move," we said.

We walked into a cold cell of a building, the kind that imprisoned people in a black and white way, not in a racist skin color sense, but in a no gray area of compassion way.

"Help, Mom, and Dad, is that you? I have been singing and deep breathing, trying to calm myself," he said.

Speet wrote his own songs, sang, and played the guitar well. I was glad at that moment for his talent. It helped him through this hell hole of a mistake.

"We are Mr. and Mrs. Patstegre, Speet's parents. What do we need to do to get our son out?" I asked.

"The bail bond is two hundred dollars to get him out. We don't take cash. You must go to the local drugstore down the street and get a cashier check. If I don't have the cashier check in my hand by 10:00 p.m. your son will have to stay overnight," Smirk Assistant said.

Mr. Patstegre and I flew out of the police station and drove to the drugstore.

Focus and floor it. Focus and floor it. We whirled Bessie into the parking lot of the only drugstore in town. We ran inside the store.

I wanted to cut everyone in line with my karate arm. Instead, I explained that I had an emergency. I found myself looking at a forty-five-year-old, weathered, cleavage exposed woman.

"I know why you are here. You need a cashier check. Here you go. Run, little lady, it's 9:45 p.m.," she said.

Our hearts hurt. Our breathing was fast. This town was choking the life out of us and our loved one.

"Come on, turn green. We must get there. We must," I said.

I tore into the building. It was 9:53 p.m. Mr. Patstegre stayed in the car, kept it running, to leave as fast as we could.

"Here is the $200 check that you asked for," I said.

I stood as tall as I could for Speet. What I saw was indescribable to a Mother.

I hugged Speet.

"I have you. It will be okay. Let's get to Bessie," I said.

"I was handcuffed, shackled, stepped on to the point where I could not breathe," Speet said.

He was bleeding from deep cuts on his wrists from the handcuffs. He was terrified.

As soon as we got into Bessie, our beautiful son was throwing his information from his wallet onto the floor of the car. Speet thought that if he got rid of his information, the Officers from Coball County would not be able to find him.

"All I did was ask for help. My stomach was on fire and I felt terrible. Why didn't they help me?" Speet asked.

"We have you now. You are safe," I answered.

There were no lights on the roads. After twenty minutes on this devil's tongue road, we finally got to the main highway. Mr. Patstegre went as fast as he could to get home.

Once inside our kitchen, the lights brought out the deep cuts on Speet's wrists and his ankles, blood on his shirt, and multiple taser marks on his chest.

"Dear God, look at our poor son. I'm trying not to lose it in front of Speet," Mr. Patstegre whispered.

"Give me your hand, my love, we will get through this together. Our love for Speet will help him in the long run. Right now, he needs us to be loving, calm, and strong. He needs to feel safe," I said.

Speet's body trembled. His anxiety accelerated into obsessive fear.

I wept everywhere except my eyes. I remained a fraud to my feelings for Speet. Love tipped the scales to one hundred percent focused attention on him and his needs.

I prayed for Speet. I looked out the window. The moon was bright. I asked the moon and the planets for support.

Saturn's rings encircled Speet every minute, every second, to try and ease his agony. I took pictures of Speet's cratered rings of blood on his wrists and ankles, twenty-six pictures in all, taken in an instant.

I used heat from Venus spinning in opposite directions to help Speet feel safe and warm. I spun on my side like Uranus to examine the rest of his body.

The light from the moon screamed out to me. "I want to help. I will be your spotlight. I see red marks of cowardness tasing on Speet's shoulder and lower chest."

That terrible night seemed like it just happened, even though it was eleven years ago. I remembered details word-for-word and action-for-action from that night.

Someday I would make things right.

Diary Entry 9 - April 7

I relived Speet's horrific encounter yesterday. Memories boiled up the hardness in me and began to crack my shell. I held my emotions in for over a decade to better care for Speet. Experts told me that I must rid myself of these emotions. No. The process of "ridness" recovery was HIPAA private, unique for me, and would be determined by me, and no one else.

I stood up. I looked in the mirror.

"I am kidnapped by rage, combined with raindrops of denial. This is my norm. I am kidnapped because no matter what I do, the frustration toward everything and everyone, is always there," I said.

I took a deep breathe.

"I am in the front row at movies trying to see straight as my neck turns up to watch the movie. I speed when I drive. Nothing makes sense and everything makes sense. I don't expect, I protect. My bellybutton rage will no longer be an inney. It will be an outey. It will act out when it chooses to. I require release. I require righteousness. I require revenge. I require dignity," I concluded.

My mind was tired. I dropped into an inviting couch of pillows and fell asleep.

Diary Entry 10 - April 10

"Get some rest" was a phrase that was said many times to tired Mothers and tired Caregivers. Kind words said with the best intentions but still said without knowing.

There was an old saying that you couldn't take care of others until you took care of yourself first. That was hard to do as a Caregiver. I tried. Tiredness usually won over self-care.

Why did Mothers after giving birth, overnight, change their appearance? The answer was when those precious bulldozers plowed their way through our bodies, our special new being, took charge of our hearts, bodies, brain, hair, and whatever else there was.

That little bulldozer dug up our sleep and our makeup routine. Combs and brushes were buried and became relics of the past. Hair clips doing the up do messy look became indented in our heads from sleeping on them.

As families grew, changing our clothes was hard because the babies' bottoms came first, then food for all, then the trimmings of school bags, clothes, combs, and brushes for the little ones, good for thee but not for me. All being done to get everyone to where they were going on time.

Returning to the house, eyeglasses were removed to curb my eager hands from doing too much.

The old-fashioned recommendations from doctors to REST meant "Remain Endlessly Stressed in Time" to me.

Diary Entry 11 - April 30

Angry thoughts retired me to bed early. I fell into a deep sleep. Underlying rage took me down an unreal mind killing dream.

I envisioned myself at a cleaning job.

In my dream, Bessie, my car, and my cleaning tools cruised twenty minutes to apartment 913. I usually cleaned in the morning. Today it was a late cleaning job, starting at about five o'clock in the afternoon.

I parked Bessie on the street. I crossed the street. I carried my cleaning friends, Vacky, my vacuum, Shiffty, my mop, and Minnet, my cleaning spray.

I strolled, humming down the sidewalk to the apartment building. I wondered how much further my cleaning job was.

I looked around and noticed a stranger approaching.

"Excuse me, my name is Fass. It looks like you work very hard. Do you feel like you are going nowhere even though you do so much? Come with me to the meeting up the street for some free food and help."

Breathing heavy, I wondered how long he had been watching me.

"I think not," I answered.

"I think not, I think not, I think not," Vacky, Shiffty, and Minnet repeated.

Our four echoing voices swallowed him up, even though Fass only heard my voice. Support from Vacky, Shiffty, and Minnet helped me through lonely and hard days. My imagination provided arms of ease, voices of luxury, and freedom from grief.

This Fass guy had a few pimples, had slime sweat dripping from his hands, and looked about thirty. He looked like something from a comic strip, flat, not real. Was he on drugs, just waiting to poison me?

"Oh, come on. You would be perfect for our group. We can offer you a new life, free food, shelter, and a life of dedicational bliss," Fass said.

"Enslave would be a better word. I know more than you think about these noodling delights that you offer. You carve with falsehoods, scare with fear, and target the brain with arrows of arrogance. Your free food and shelter are code for drugged infused drinks that hold young and old without having to use shackles or cages," I said.

Fass sickened me. My stomach twirled like a baton being thrown up in the air, falling and then bouncing from one side of my stomach to the other instead of being caught. It raised my blood pressure.

This Fass creature, that appeared in my dream, time-triggered me backwards and gave me Flash-Gordon style strength.

I had a motto of Don't Take Things to Heart - DTTH. Most people said not to take things personally. I preferred using my motto. It worked most of the time. It did not work on Fass because his words tricked innocence, manipulated kindness, and were filled with deceit.

His words glue-gunned to me.

One speck of spit shadiness from Fass and I was in the high anxiety realism of Speet's trauma.

Fass wanted to abduct innocence, control, and char minds.

Fass interrupted my thoughts.

"I am so sorry that you have been led astray by untrue information. Nothing you said is true. We do not do any of those things that you mentioned. Come with me and I will show you the way," Fass said.

"Fass, you and other evildoers control young adults and children until you punch card them out," I said.

I pictured similar words had circled Speet's head as he remained captive in a world of deceit. I needed to stop this lying, horrible Fass just like I wished I could have stopped the evil man who abused our son, Speet. Kidnapping, drugging, and abusing young adults was wicked.

"Follow me, Fass, to my car, Bessie. I need to put my cleaning tools in the back. We can continue our talk there," I said.

I walked to Bessie. Fass obeyed and followed. I opened the back door of Bessie. I put Vacky, Shiffty, and Minnet on the ground. They were smiling at me, hoping they would be able to help. Vacky, an upright citizen standing four feet tall, had an arm handle that could do many things besides sucking. She was my watchdog, my protector. Strategic and futuristic Shiffty guided me and was with me all the way. Minnet sprayed her magic when needed.

"Fass, can you help put things in the back of Bessie?" I asked.

"Of course," Fass said.

As Fass started to bend down to help put my cleaning supplies in Bessie, Vacky screamed, "You twit, you tried to inject me with a date rape drug when I wasn't looking."

Standing tall, Vacky hit Fass's face. He fell, bleeding, face down. We picked up Fass and threw him into Bessie.

Vacky hopped into the back of Bessie. Vacky swung her tippity top handle with concrete certainness at Fass's body. Blood sprayed everywhere. Minnet and Shiffty stuffed cotton rags in Fass's mouth to stop him from screaming.

"Hit, hit, hit, smack, smack, smack, that's how we spend the day away in the merry old land of Mrs. Patstegre," Vacky sang as she mutilated Fass.

Fass was evil. He needed to be stopped from hurting others. That look alike and act alike Image of God was a stealer of life; a thief robbing innocence from the vulnerable.

Vacky and I put Fass inside a large duffle bag. He was dead. I put Shiffty and Minnet into the far back of Bessie. I moved Vacky and the duffle bag with Fass inside to Bessie's second row seats. I wanted Vacky to watch the bag until we got to where we were going.

It was dark outside. I climbed back into Bessie and grabbed the wheel. I put the second-row seat window down next to Vacky so she could have air.

I decided to take Fass to the river at the edge of town.

"Here we go, Bessie," I said.

I pressed the pedal and sped toward the river. I took a sharp turn. Bessie jumped on the sidewalk making the Fass-bag lean out the open window smacking a lamppost. I thought the bag might split open. It didn't. Bessie was a large car. Even after all these years of Bessie and I being together, I had not mastered taking tight turns.

We arrived at the river. I took a deep breathe while looking into the clear water. I saw three beautiful fish swimming around. I threw the bag with Fass inside toward the fish.

"Please take this bait and chew hard. Disperse the rest to the hungry in the sea until it is gone," I said.

I crowned myself and knighted my friends, Vacky, Shiffty, and Minnet. Maybe that was enough. Maybe it wasn't. Maybe that was enough. Maybe it wasn't. The petals of tomorrow would tell.

As I sat in Bessie, Minnet spun in circles and sprayed things spotless. Before I knew it, we were all clean.

I drove home. Music played. The night was calm.

I sat up in my bed. I paused. I looked around my room. I sighed. This mind killing of Fass was a bad dream.

"Praise me Father for I have sinned, in my thoughts. I have committed deeds of hatred. I do these things, Oh Lord, because of harm inflicted on innocence by evil manipulators. I envision actions of righteousness done by Caregivers over lawn mower, empowered people who run over the blameless and inflict pain.

"Dear God, no Hail Marys, or Our Fathers as penance for me. I am a complex person, guided and misguided by love. The music created by loved ones with mental illness is beautiful if people would take time to listen to the person, rather than the illness. Sometimes, chaotic thinking is genius in disguise and pain that needs no disguise. Please be with me as I follow, defend, and care for others. Amen," I said out loud.

I stood up from my bed. I thought to myself. Why didn't God let me kill despicable Fass in real life? Would it have been better than mind killing Fass?

No.

Mind killing let me experience undisturbed disgust without consequences from a cold world. It provided dignity to my frustration so that I could continue Caregiving for Speet and others.

My hurt heart and protective Caregiving wanted evildoers to feel the pain that we saw loved ones suffer and live with every day.

Diary Entry 12 - May 5

I slept on and off for days after experiencing my mind killing dream of Fass.

Would that nightmare bump me up and down off the curbs of life? Would I become a more complicated network of angry mazes than I already was? I didn't know.

I did know that it was time for a day at Concerned Care Nursing Home.

"Good morning, Crystal."

"Hello, Mrs. Patstegre," Crystal said.

I saw something dangle from Crystal's wrist.

"Look at that. A bracelet with a heart charm screams boyfriend to me. Am I right?" I asked.

"Yes, his name is Percy. He wants to be a doctor. We motivate each other to learn considering we are both studying to work in the medical field. Who knows, I may even decide to become a doctor instead of a nurse," Crystal answered.

"I'm happy for you," I said.

"Thanks, Mrs. Patstegre. See you when you are finished," Crystal said.

In between greeting people at the receptionist desk, Crystal studied for classes.

Recently, Concerned Care Nursing Home hired Crystal to work a couple of days a week. Her job helped her with expenses for nursing school. She worked around her classes. She even offered a helping hand and a smile to the wonderful elderly that lived at Concerned Care during her breaks.

Today, I stacked my cart with magazines like *People* and *Time*. I also brought newspapers such as *The Wall Street Journal, The New York Times,* and some local papers. I put some pens, pencils, pads of paper, and medically approved snacks on the cart, too.

"Good morning, Care-Cart Lady," said a passing nurse.

"Good morning," I replied.

I wheeled my cart down the hall and handed out whatever the residents wanted. I talked with the residents as much as they wanted me to, depending on their moods.

I got to Ms. File's room. Her door was open. I peaked in.

"Good morning, Ms. File," I said.

Ms. File was sitting in an old black rocker, moving back and forth.

"Oh, so glad to see you again, Mrs. Patstegre. We had a nice talk last time you were here," Ms. File said.

"I have *The Wall Street Journal* for you if you want it," I said.

"I would love it. Do you have a *New York Times*?" Ms. File asked.

"I do. You can have both. I know how much you like to stay on top of what is going on in the world. Once a teacher, always a teacher. I am sure you know more than most with your love of learning," I answered.

"Any former students planning to visit you today, Ms. File?" I asked.

"I don't know. They drop by whenever they have time. They know that they are the only family I have. I hope their visits continue until the Lord wants his own history lesson," Ms. File answered.

We both laughed.

"Have you painted any new paintings?" I asked.

"No, Mrs. Patstegre, my hands have been bothering me. The doctors think it is arthritis. We are trying different medications and physical therapy. Hopefully, that will help. I want to get back to creating," Ms. File answered.

"I am sorry. I'll pray something starts to help. Have a good day, Ms. File. It was nice to see you again," I said.

"God bless you, Mrs. Patstegre. As Alex Haley said, 'Anytime you see a turtle on top of a fence post, you know he had some help,'" Ms. File said.

What a grand and clever lady, Ms. File was. Next time, I would bring a quote and ask Ms. File who said it.

I traveled in and out of the residents' rooms. Some were sleeping. I left their medically approved snacks on a side table along with a magazine or two.

"Hey, are you planning on skipping me? Why should I think people would be kind here," said a gruff voice from a room with an open door.

"I'm sorry. My list says that no one lives in your room number. I am Mrs. Patstegre, the Care-Cart Lady. You must be new here," I said.

I used my DTTH - Don't Take Things to Heart motto. His gruffness bounced off me. I focused on the reason behind his abrupt words.

So many people lived at Concerned Care Nursing Home because their family could not work it out for them to stay in their own home. They were aging fast. Many were in pain, scared, and lonely. It was sad to watch the dignity, respect, kindness, compassion, and care that those lovely elderly people deserved being exchanged for the hand of impatient and noncaring relatives. I was determined to give them the care and respect they deserved when I was there.

"I am. I'm not very happy to be new here. My kids are too self-centered to help me figure out a way to stay in my own house. They don't value an aging parent. Respect is shown for older people in other countries. People in those countries would shun children that take their parents out of their home and put them into a place like this," the gruff man said.

My heart felt for him. This man needed someone to listen to him.

"Well, Mr. um, I didn't catch your name," I said.

"I'm G. Gaudan, last name rhymes with sedan. I was a businessman, husband, and father. My family will tell you, if they would ever come around, that I lived my life wearing those three hats. My wife of fifty-five years died a few years ago. I have a son and a daughter who lead busy lives with their wives and children. Hell, everyone is busy. Day Care is on the rise, time after work is limited, and weekend hours are never enough.

"I yearn for the old days when relatives opened their houses to family members that needed help and spent time with each other," G. Gaudan said.

My cart opened more than doors to rooms. It allowed me to use my intuition and insight to pay attention to the residents. I tried to help them with whatever they needed.

"Mr. Gaudan, I yearn for the old days, too.

"I'm sorry but I don't have a snack with your name on it since you just moved in. I could ask the nurse to get you one if you would like me to. Would you like a newspaper, magazine, or any of the other things that you see on the cart?" I asked.

"I do not want a snack. I'll take *The Wall Street Journal*," Mr. Gaudan answered.

"Here you go. It was nice to meet you. I look forward to getting to know you better," I said.

Mr. Gaudan started reading his newspaper. I slipped out of his room without him noticing.

I was determined to get into all the rooms before the day was done.

I returned my Care-Cart when I finished.

I waved goodbye to Crystal.

"See you soon," I said.

"Bye, Mrs. Patstegre," Crystal said.

Diary Entry 13 - May 13

Speet and I drank coffee in our kitchen. Nicked cherry cabinets, plant stands full of plants, and plenty of light adorned the room. We sat on wooden backed stools with thatched seats. Speet and I elbowed together on a gray, white, and hint of green granite counter. Speet stared out the window.

"Are you going to your therapist today?" I asked.

Speet nodded yes.

Speet told me nothing about his visits to his therapist, Dr. Sible. I respected his privacy and their connectedness.

Speet took a sip of his coffee.

"Can I take your car for my appointment? My car needs some work. I haven't felt like taking it in," Speet asked.

"Sure. Bessie would love it," I answered.

I handed Speet my keys. Speet smiled when he saw the gray, fluffy pom-pom attached to the key chain. I smiled back with my cheerleading eyes.

"Have a nice session. See you when you get home," I said.

"Thanks for letting me use Bessie," Speet said.

I sat down after Speet left. I felt restless and nauseous. That sick feeling caused me to punch everyone and everything through words in my diary. My disgust brought dignity to the validity of what I wrote.

I decided I needed to talk to someone.

I called my good friend, Clippy. Our friendship was formed long ago from school function togetherness. Clippy and I chaired parties and sporting events - Clippy's daughter and Speet were good at sports and good friends at school.

Clippy's diamond studded heart was priceless. Her blond hair, sometimes sporting different color highlights, and tan skin were opposite my dark hair and fair skin. Loss, caring, and intensity connected us.

"What's up, Dawg!" Clippy said.

"Clippy, it is impossible to communicate anything when no one wants to listen. Exaggerated emotions and reclusive air are two balls that I catch and desensitize during my day," I said.

"I feel that way, too, Mrs. Patstegre. Good thing I understand you and your words. You do think too much. All this pain you have needs to get the hell knocked out of it," Clippy said.

"I knew you would cheer me up with your refreshing self, Clippy," I said.

"What else is on your mind, Mrs. Patstegre?" Clippy asked.

"I love the game of Bingo. I replace the "o" with an "e" and I get Binge. Fatness is all around me. I am smothering in it," I said.

"Why do you talk that way, Mrs. Patstegre? So, you eat. Who cares. I eat and I don't care. You are too hard on yourself," Clippy said.

"Clippy, women in the past were attractive with curves. Curves were sought after. Don't the women who starve on the tread mills of life and cut, cut, snip, snip their bodies to please themselves and the vainness of their mates end up disappointed? Their mates that prefer perceived perfection will find a younger woman when the older woman's petals fall off," I said.

"Hell, yes, they will. Look at my bastard of a husband. He wagged his tail everywhere and at everyone that would grab it. Not saying I'm a beauty queen, but I am. Men are babies. They need so much cuddling or is it coddling or is it both? I don't want a man and I don't need one," Clippy said.

"Clippy, most men have a "get to the point" attitude when they speak. I think it's a gene they are born with," I said.

"You said it. Hey, Mrs. Patstegre, I must run to the grocery store. Call you later," Clippy said.

"Alright. Love you," I said.

"See ya, love ya more," Clippy said.

I hung up. Injustice molded both of us. Soon our molds would crack.

Diary Entry 14 - June 3

My sister Effie and I agreed to work on her apartment tomorrow at eight o'clock in the morning via Facetime or speaker phone. Her apartment was small. She decided she wanted my help to figure out what to give away or throw away but not my physical appearance in her apartment. She was unpredictable. Doing it her way was the best way.

Effie carried scars from bad relationships that made her question her intuition and her ability to pick good guys.

Effie had fifty-year-old skin minus the wrinkles. She had a beautiful face. Effie worked jobs of equal caliber; each job tooted with her youthful appearance. She would like to wax off extra pounds, who wouldn't. Cognitive of the need for change, she was afraid of it.

Effie suffered from octogen perfection, the art of procrastination.

Once Effie got traction and got the hang of something new, she became good at it.

Diary Entry 15 - June 4

I called Effie, at eight o'clock in the morning, like we agreed. I wanted to get our day started.

"Hello," Effie said.

"Good morning. Giddy up, giddy up, no trotting today," I said.

"I'm still in bed. The parrot talked all night. I am going to get the apartment in order, work on it today by myself," Effie said.

"Okay. Can we at least attack your closet over the phone, like we talked about the other day?" I asked.

"We can tandem around your abode that houses your comfort through our voices on speaker phone. I love you. I know our relationship can be like a swing set. Some days slide up. Some days slide down. Swinging together can be high, low, fast, or slow with nice glides in between," I said.

"I tried to understand all of that. I'm too tired right now. Maybe after I feed my sweet parrot, Pepper, and take a shower, we can do some work together either in person or by phone," Effie said.

"Okay," I said.

I whispered to myself, "Your job, Mrs. Patstegre, is to take the impossible mission, if you so choose, of breaking a ten-year bicycle ride down memory lane that she lives in. Effie has it in her to be a Tour de France Champion, if she chooses."

We hung up. I had a conversation with myself. How much time did it take to clean out one large closet and two smaller ones? Certainly not years.

In the past, I weakened and tempered out at her. Wasn't right, not proud of it, and it wasn't productive. I said I was sorry. She said she was sorry. We went on.

Sometimes she was the engine, and I was the caboose. Then we switched. Today I would have settled for us being two cars in between the engine and caboose, anything to help her move forward.

An hour passed. I called again.

"Hi, Effie. I have tools. You have desire. We have time. Let's juggle in person or over the phone. Jump into my place, and I will jump into yours. Let's jump together. Trampoline up, grab a dress, fly it through the air, and land the dress into your give away bag of freedom, an emancipation," I said.

"I will try. How about three this afternoon on speaker phone?" Effie asked.

"OOOOOkkkkkkkaaaaaayyyyy," I said.

Three o'clock in the afternoon became three o'clock in the morning without any jumping. Gone were days of winded sentences and labor pleading, I thought. I knew I would not stay true to that thought.

I needed sleep.

I had a phone interview with a potential cleaning client tomorrow, or was it in a couple of days?

Diary Entry 16 - June 6

The phone rang before the mugginess of my day started.

"Hello," I said.

"My name is Sem Bok. I'm looking for Mrs. Patstegre. I have an interview with her for a deep cleaning for my house."

I got right into the interview.

"This is Mrs. Patstegre. How many family members are there in your household and how many bedrooms and baths do you have?"

I wanted to say how many biting babies, smart mouthed teenagers, and animals, do you have, but I didn't.

"I have a husband and two girls. I have three bedrooms and two baths. It is a typical house," Sem Bok said.

Not when I got through with your house, I thought to myself. My curious hands wandered into areas where they shouldn't.

"Sem, I will clean for you September 8 at nine o'clock in the morning. I give you a deep cleaning. I don't come back. I am what you call a get your house back on track cleaner," I said.

"Will that work for you?" I asked.

Sem gobbled up the date and time.

Diary Entry 17 - August 29

Speet and I ate dinner out tonight. Our food was delicious. Our conversation flowed.

We drove home in Bessie. We went upstairs and said good night to each other.

"Oh, Speet, before you go to bed, may I run something by you?" I asked.

"Sure Mom," Speet answered.

I went into my room and grabbed a piece of paper with what I wanted Speet to listen to. I went into Speet's room.

"Speet, helpful words flow to my brain while caring for people. Mind Binders is the name I awarded to these spontaneous thoughts. There are seven of them that I would like to share with you," I said.

"Okay, go ahead. I'm listening," Speet said.

"Here are the Mind Binders:

- o Caregiving is not enabling. It is easy to call a Caregiver an enabler. It is hard for the accuser to defend that statement.

- o I see tigers instead of cats. I see wolves instead of dogs. Strength and power are needed for movement and advocacy.

- o Words from grief are really words of painful praise. The person suffering from anxiety or depression chooses us to listen to them. We are the lucky ones to have been chosen.

- o Know when to boundary up. Know when to boundary down.

- o Loved ones who suffer from mental illness can combine their drive, coping skills, and desire to feel better along with their Caregiver's drive, experience, and intuition to form a strategic edge to outrun the symptoms of mental illness.

o   Plant bulbs and watch them blossom into tulips of
    emotions.

o   A Caregiver's heart causes other hearts to keep
    beating."

"I like them, Mom. I especially like the last two," Speet
said.

"Thanks for listening. Have a nice sleep," I said.

Speet smiled.

"You sleep well, too," Speet said.

Diary Entry 18 - September 8

Anger and hate boxed each other inside of me. I'm not sure
why they did. Don't they mean the same thing?

Mental illness stole relationships, employment, and
enjoyment from loved ones. People suffering from mental
illness dealt with dread and lava around their beds, darts in
their shower, and furrowed fears.

Loved ones rode bareback and fell for decades, hoping for
that true stable saddle to appear and help them. Why
couldn't the medical world find cures for "Jack the Ripper"
illnesses, such as Anxiety, Depression, PTSD, Bipolar
Disorder, and Schizophrenia?

"News flash for the futuristic and strategic politician –
spotlight the persecuted group, the mentally ill and the
homeless, accelerate change for mental illness as your truth

title, and you will lift yourself from a nobody to a member of Congress or even the Presidency," I said out loud.

This morning as I laid in bed, I realized that this boxing match of anger and hate gave me strength.

My strength took me to another cleaning job. I was going to the Bok's house to clean.

I hopped into Bessie with Vacky, Shiffty, and Minnet.

"Bessie, I am a sizzling, happy, confused, angry, and comforting Caregiver," I said as I drove to the Bok's cleaning job.

Many times, I talked to Bessie. It amused me and made driving exciting. Safety screamed security to me behind her wheel of age and support.

I arrived at the Boks.

I lifted the mat to get the key. The Bok family left it for me. It was milkman delivery time. I went in.

"It's me. I'm here to clean," I called out.

Sem Bok entered the foyer.

"Good morning, it is nice to meet you. Have some coffee or help yourself to whatever you want. You can start in our room, the largest bedroom. My better half is already at work. I'll be out of your way soon," Sem Bok said.

"That's fine. I'll lock up when I finish. I will leave your key on the kitchen counter," I said.

"C'mon kids. We must go. Here's your vegan lunches and your hand sanitizer," Sem Bok said.

Sem, and her two girls jumped in the car like flees. Their dog of a car barked down the driveway dribbling pee. The Boks misunderstood my fake nice face. It wasn't nice. It was a face of survival, not of the fittest, but of the necessary. I worked, I did, I acted, and I finished. I laid in the dirt, smiled with the worms, and swam with reverb. Everything was muffled to the tune of who I used to be.

Rage was low on the temperature gage from the strength talk I had with myself this morning. Rage gage, I liked that. I breezed cleaned the house with Vacky, my vacuum, Shiffty, my mop, and Minnet, my cleaning spray at my side. My team of make believe had many tricks to clean. Today, we used every one of them.

I decided I would be an appetizing nuisance today.

"Now to the kitchen. Let's dialogue. Music to words. I hate being this nice. I'm gagey ragey, not killy willy today. Focus on the rhyme and not the crime today. Rhyming might lower the boxing match of hate and anger that thrives in me," I said out loud.

I opened the refrigerator.

"Here peachy, peachy...oh here kiddy, kiddy. This might appease my gagey ragey if I wasn't so cool in front of the refrigerator. Remember this is not a killy, willy day. Be nice," I said.

"What do you want with me, master, I do not want to be hurt by you," a peach whimpered.

"Don't worry, peachy, weachy. I am going to slowpoke with the Coke and invade the parade of pristine vegan smiles. Take this salami, and that pepperoni, and this ham on your pure skins of sappy apples, parrot talking carrots, and dead bread…had to get dead in there somewhere. You vegan pristines need Listerine now.

"I'm going shelf to shelf to make you all think I am the ultimate smasher and masher, gobbler of cobbler, and sucker of Smuckers," I said.

"I'll get you my yummy little things," I laughed.

"Please don't. Please stop," they all screamed.

"Hey, you all got off lucky today. I, Mrs. Patstegre of Nottingham, paid you a visit and arrowed your identity, not your life. Now shut up, don't blabby flabby your mouths to the cocky Boks, and be happy that I did not skin and eat you all alive," I said.

I closed the ceiling to floor refrigerator's door. I concluded my fun food fantasy.

I grabbed Vacky, Shiffty, and Minnet and left.

"Can humor reach levels of serotonin as fulfilling as antidepressants? Can humor laugh and cry at the same time?" I questioned out loud as Bessie and I drove home.

Diary Entry 19 - September 9

I would not allow gravity grief to nail me to non-movement.

My love for Speet and others flew me high above a cupola of buried feelings. Caregiving lifted my head, actions, heart, body, and thought process all the time. Watching Speet suffer pain more than the normal marks of growth on the wall, put me into a World's Fair of unfairness.

Diary Entry 20 - September 10

Target practice was on my mind this morning. I imagined a dart board with the outer ring broad and round. The outer ring was stigma and discrimination. The next ring going toward the bullseye was anxiety and depression. The next inner ring was the justice system sending people exhibiting mental health symptoms in public to jail. The bullseye was all the people that called Caregivers, enablers.

Every time someone threw a dart on this board, wherever it fell, it lessened distress for loved ones suffering from mental illness.

Diary Entry 21 - September 11

Fall coming, cold coming, homeless freezing, and food needed, sparked me to put my talents to use for hungry and homeless people. I signed up to cook at a soup kitchen called Hookum. Hookum was about fifteen minutes from my house.

I loaded up Bessie and drove to Hookum. The volunteer agency instructed me to arrive at eleven in the morning. The door would be open. The head of volunteers would lock up after I left. A volunteer would be there to help me serve.

I parked near a shabby brick building with a small wooden sign dangling from rusty chains. The sign had Hook minus the um on it.

I walked into a cold, low lit, and unwelcoming kitchen. A shadow of a figure approached me.

"Hi, I'm Gus. I am volunteering here for college credit."

"My name is Mrs. Patstegre," I said.

This college boy, Gus, stared at me; I guessed he was wondering what to say.

"What food did you bring, Mrs. Patstegre?" Gus asked.

"I brought pasta with my homemade white sauce and vegetables," I answered.

"Sounds great. What made you decide to volunteer to help and serve the homeless?" Gus asked.

"I want to show the homeless that they are deserving of a home cooked meal. Some of the homeless are educated people who lost good jobs and traded a desk for the ground. Many homeless suffer from mental illness and run with no place to go. Veterans suffer from Post-Traumatic Stress Disorder – PTSD. Their symptoms can drive them to homelessness. Some of the homeless suffer from addiction and abuse," I answered.

I thought to myself for a moment. Why didn't any of the under wearing, guard protected elite politicians see the homeless and the mentally ill? Did the need to win their elections blind them from seeing the homeless? How many homeless voted? Was a vote more important than the well-being of the mentally ill and the homeless?

I noticed when I saw and talked with the homeless that their eyes sang in unison. They all had purpose when they started out in life. The break-a-leg good luck slogan did not work for them. Sameness, hopelessness, and poverty settled in. They pinched privacy whenever possible. No one yearned for this. No one wanted this. This was what they got when they crossed the border of their previous life and headed to nomad, homeless land.

Gus startled me and my thoughts when he stuck his finger in my pasta sauce and tasted it.

"How do you make such a delicious dish?" Gus asked.

"Do you really want to know?" I asked.

"Yes, believe it or not, I like to cook when I get the chance," Gus answered.

"I use eight tablespoons of butter, six heaping tablespoons of flour, one cup of vegie or chicken broth and three cups or more of cream per sixteen ounces of cooked pasta. I steam vegetables and toss them with the pasta. I made twelve sixteen-ounce batches for today," I said.

"Wow, you really do make food from scratch for the homeless," Gus said.

"Yes, I do. Speaking of my food, I brought a couple pans of pasta in when I first came. I would appreciate it if you might bring in the rest of the food from my car. It's the cream-colored SUV parked right in front of Hookum. Here are the keys," I said.

"I'm on it, Mrs. Patstegre," Gus said.

Gus carried all the food in. I put the pans of pasta in two very large double ovens in the kitchen.

Gus seemed older than a college kid. He wore an inquisitive coat that most college students did not wear.

"Gus let's get things ready. Our guests will be coming soon," I said.

"Mrs. Patstegre, you referred to the homeless as our guests. Who does that?" Gus asked.

"I do. They deserve respect. They deserve kindness. They deserve love. They deserve employment. These are rights that need to be repeated. I call them repetition rights. They each have their own useful uniqueness which could be tech ability, music, care skills, business skills, humor, intelligence, wit, and the like," I answered.

There were many rectangular tables with eight or so chairs around each table. One of those long tables had a stack of white tablecloths on it.

Gus and I put the tablecloths on all the tables. They draped halfway to the floor. We put paper napkins, forks, and coffee on a table in the corner of the large dining room. Gus found live plants on a table in the sun. He put one plant on each of the rectangular tables.

"Here come our guests. I will plate the main course and salad on glass plates that I found in the kitchen. Why don't you add two chocolate chip cookies to their plates and hand a bottle of water to each guest. They can get the coffee, napkins, and forks themselves from the corner table," I said.

So many of the homeless had a stare of hopelessness. Their eyes sliced me as sharp as the knives I used to prepare their meal. I served them with pride.

I looked at Gus. He was busy putting dessert on plates and handing out bottles of water.

"How is college these days, Gus?" I asked.

"College is fine," Gus answered.

"Is it hard to be yourself on campus? Why do others think they should be able to interrupt your hues and values for you. How do students deal with being on guard most of the time?" I asked.

"I find out what my professors' views are in the beginning of each semester. It doesn't hurt to know. I still have my own views and thoughts. I am just more discreet with them. Some students are more vocal than me. However, most agree that there is too much power in the hands of a few," Gus answered.

Our last guest left. I hoped that my eyes of compassion expressed and celebrated uniqueness in each homeless person that I served and talked with today.

"You do so much, Mrs. Patstegre. You do it with grace and manners. You make these homeless people feel like they are special," Gus said.

"They are special, Gus. You will see for yourself one day if you keep an open mind and keep volunteering," I said.

We cleaned up. Most of the food went. Everyone had a meal together, sat at the tables, and accomplished the art of eating with very little acting out.

Gus threw away napkins and paper coffee cups left on tables. Then he grabbed the tablecloths, ripping them off the tables like a magician. I collected all my bowls and pans.

I was told to leave the dirty tablecloths on the table closest to the front door.

"Gus, can you please help me carry my pans and bowls to my car," I asked.

"Sure," Gus answered.

Bessie, my trusted car, waited patiently for me. She perked up when she saw me.

Gus and I gave a quick wave to each other.

Diary Entry 22 - September 12

I was tired from volunteering at the Hookum Soup Kitchen yesterday. I decided to go to bed early tonight.

Gus had secrets. I carried secrets so I knew when others did.

I laid on my bed. It was nine o'clock in the evening.

"Mrs. Patstegre, you look tired. It appears that you are working or caring for people most of the time," a voice said.

"Who said that? Did I imagine a voice?" I asked out loud.

I heard a slight creak. Magically, two eyes popped open on my bedroom ceiling. I sat up, then laid back down on my bed.

"Are you talking to me, ceiling? Do I really have a Talking Ceiling in my bedroom?" I asked.

"You do. I have been watching over you. I'm now talking to you. You have deep sorrow and sadness beneath your hardness, beneath your dark brown hair, and beneath your big brown eyes. Your buried emotions are magnetic," Talking Ceiling answered.

I liked the perceptiveness of Talking Ceiling.

"Trigger spells, trigger spells, trigger all the way. Trigger spells what? Trigger spells nightmare. Trigger spells misunderstanding. Trigger spells agony as what is to come," I said.

I don't know why I mumbled these little jingles. Maybe they soothed me.

"Talking Ceiling, behind symptoms of defense mechanism darts, displaced distancing of understanding, and dice throwing moods from a loved one suffering, there is a smile, sad eyes, a hug, or some other sign that drops a dew of cognitive love on my face. It is a force that moves me in a way that is unexplainable," I said.

Talking Ceiling didn't say anything. Maybe she was taking in everything I just said.

"Talking Ceiling, thanks for listening."

"You are very welcome. Goodnight, Mrs. Patstegre. May you have calm thoughts and fall fast asleep," Talking Ceiling said.

I turned on my side. I closed my eyes. The slightest hint of a tear fell from my face. I wondered when my next mind kill would be. Why did my fury cause me to mind kill in my dreams? Maybe releasing deep emotions was the reason.

Entry 23 - September 13

I woke up early. I dragged myself around most of the day, not understanding why I was still tired. I talked with Speet, paid bills, watched a couple of shows, and decided it was a stay-at-home day.

Speet and I had a quick dinner. He played music in his room. I joined Talking Ceiling, my new creative channel of conversation in my bedroom.

"Talking Ceiling, I am going to watch television and go to bed early tonight," I said.

"That is a good idea. Fall asleep during one of your shows and I will turn your television off," Talking Ceiling said.

After about twenty minutes, I fell into a deep sleep. I found myself descending into another mind killing dream.

In my dream, I called Clippy.

"What's up, Dawg!" Clippy said.

"What's up, Clippy, is my uncontrolled resentment. I fear the mold protecting my buried feelings is cracking and nothing will stay silent.

"My vindictiveness fills me with desires to stab, punch, and mind kill. I want to rebel against a life the norm call reality. The ignorance believed by most people about mental illness needs tutoring. I'm attracted to an old-fashioned eye-for-an-eye and an appetite that is satisfied without food," I said.

"Mrs. Patstegre, I say let's get revenge against an evil, lying drug dealer," Clippy said.

"Clippy, let's whirl around with Zorro's cape and the Lone Ranger's mask, painting goodness. Goodness in our minds, badness to the minds and bodies of deviants," I said.

"Mrs. Patstegre, I lost my niece, Amber, to a fentanyl overdose. She got addicted to fentanyl in college from her boyfriend who was a dealer. His name was Norman. She dropped out of college.

"Amber's days were filled with abuse, suffering, and horror. Amber battled depression. Instead of her boyfriend helping her find a good therapist/psychiatrist, he gave her drugs. She self-medicated to numb her depression. Many times, addiction starts from being mentally ill.

"Last time I saw my niece, she was in a hospital, beaten and raped. I barely recognized her. She had a broken jaw, swollen shut eyes, and a bruised body. A couple days later she passed away," Clippy said.

"Clippy, drug dealers destroy lives. Fentanyl pushers are fake chess players that think their moves always win.

"Clippy, I went through a similar trauma. I had a nephew, Ivan, who lost his life to fentanyl poisoning at the young age of twenty-eight. He was successful in business, enjoyed life, and volunteered in his community. He suffered from anxiety.

"Ivan ran out of his prescription, Xanax, which helped tame his anxiety. His friend, Jasper, gave him a pill which was a look-alike prescription Xanax. Jasper had no idea that the pills he gave Ivan had fentanyl in them.

"Jasper heard Ivan vomiting late at night. He thought Ivan was coming down with the flu. The next morning, he went into Ivan's room because Ivan's dog needed to go outside. Jasper couldn't wake him up. He touched Ivan. Ivan's body felt cold. Jasper didn't think Ivan was breathing. He called 911. The paramedics pronounced Ivan dead," I said.

"That is awful, Mrs. Patstegre. I think we should find a fentanyl drug dealer and abuse him like he destroyed my niece and your nephew. These drug dealers not only get young adults addicted to fentanyl, but they are also responsible for poisoning loved ones by putting fentanyl in look-alike prescription pills," Clippy said.

"Clippy, rumors on the streets of Ladin, where the homeless live, say there is a drug dealer, Dr. Epy who has a side kick, Norman. These two, along with their gang are responsible for selling fentanyl and hurting many in this area. I wonder if this is the same Norman that killed your niece? There is a good chance he is. Dr. Epy kills the innocent with his drugs. Norman, nicknamed the Puncher, bullies people into taking drugs and abuses girls when he pleases," I said.

Clippy and I wanted justice from injustice. Our intuition moved the Ouija board to spell "Fairness" tonight.

"Clippy, we can release our fury toward these fentanyl killers. I will pick you up at midnight," I said.

"I'm in Mrs. Patstegre," Clippy said.

"Great. Bye, Clippy. See you soon,"

"Bye, Mrs. Patstegre."

I arrived at Clippy's house at eleven thirty at night. I tooted Bessie's horn. Clippy ran out.

"Hi Clippy. We are headed to Ladin. I found out information from a person who volunteers for the homeless about Dr. Epy and Norman. Dr. Epy is bald, short, and walks with a limp. Norman is almost six feet tall. He usually wears an old, olive-green army jacket and a red baseball cap. They are known to hang out at Tiggles, a bar.

"Clippy, we will help the people of Ladin by getting rid of two wicked deviants," I said.

"Mrs. Patstegre, I am ready to help," Clippy said.

We arrived in Ladin. Clippy and I parked close to Tiggles Bar. We saw a guy wearing a red baseball cap smoking a cigarette outside the bar. He fit Norman's description. Dr. Epy shouldn't be far behind. Hopefully, their gang followers were barking elsewhere tonight.

"Clippy, a small, bald, man walking with a limp, just came out of Tiggles. He is talking to Norman. That must be Dr. Epy. We found the two criminals," I said.

Dr. Epy and Norman walked to their car. Dr. Epy got in the passenger side. Norman got behind the wheel of a black Mercedes. They drove off. We followed. I thought about slamming Bessie into them and forcing them off the road. As much as the devilish pair deserved Bessie plowing into them, I did not want Bessie to get hurt.

We continued to follow them. They parked in front of a house. We parked about fifty feet behind them. This seemed too easy.

We got out of the car. Clippy and I looked at each other and took out firecrackers, knives, hammers, and a few tasers that we brought with us. We lit a pack of firecrackers and threw them at Dr. Epy and Norman as they got out of their car. Clippy and I thought for sure they would start shooting. They didn't.

Instead, the cowards, Norman, and Dr. Epy, took a good look at us. Norman started yelling.

"What pathetic amateurs, throwing firecrackers instead of shooting real bullets. Why would women like you, take us on and want to die a painful death?"

I thought, weren't all deaths painful?

Hand Puncher Norman stood in front of Bessie.

"You want me, bitches?" Norman said.

"We sure do. We will kick your sorry ass," said Clippy.

We tip-toed toward the front of Bessie.

Dr. Epy and Hand Puncher Norman yelled and threatened us. Suddenly, Norman grabbed a woman walking by and began to assault her.

"Help, help me," the woman screamed.

Bessie heard. In two seconds, she raised her eyelash blades. They became high powered water hoses. Bessie beamed her lights toward Norman and aimed the water hoses toward his eyes. The water pressure knocked Norman down on the ground bleeding and watering himself, giving the attacked woman time to get away. Norman flapped around, trying to get up. He was directionally disabled due to Bessie's headlights and the force of her powerful water hoses.

For the first time Bessie acted out in front of others. Clippy, delighted, went along with the action.

"Mrs. Patstegre, here is a hammer for you," Clippy said.

While Norman the Hand Puncher slithered around on the ground, Clippy and I took turns hitting his body. Blood spurted everywhere. Blows were given for the drug induced, mentally ill, and homeless that Puncher Norman had bullied, violated, and killed.

We continued cracking bones in Norman's hands, his weapon of choice, that hurt so many. Now his deformed fingers would be useless weapons if he lived. We looked around for Dr. Epy and saw him run into his house.

"You coward, get over here," Clippy screamed.

We ran to a one-story brick house with black shutters. What a joke! Where was the white picket fence?

We carried weapons, powerful alone, deadly when revenge was the cherry on top.

Clippy and I tied one end of a rope to the doorknob of Dr. Epy's front door of his house. We then tied the other end to Bessie's front bumper. I drove in reverse. Down came the door. I put Bessie in park. Clippy and I jumped over the threshold. Clippy ran one way. I ran the other.

"I found him. He is hiding under the bed. Balk. Balk. You have made this too easy," Clippy said.

With amazing strength, Clippy dragged Dr. Epy out. She picked him up and threw him to the ground.

I walked in the room. Clippy and I stepped on Dr. Epy's hands with our heavy work boots. We heard bones crack. We moved our feet in back-and-forth movements, like we were putting out cigarettes, crushing more of his bones.

"Clippy, make Dr. Epy take this sedative."

"Okay, Mrs. Patstegre."

"I have an idea. Let's tie these ropes around Dr. Epy's ankles and wrists. I will tie the leg ropes to Bessie. Clippy, tie the wrist ropes around the legs of that large, heavy mahogany chest of drawers," I said.

After all the knots were tied, I put Bessie in reverse, and pressed the gas pedal. Suddenly, Bessie and I heard screams from the rotten coward, Dr. Epy. His legs slide off like well-done chicken falling off the bones. One leg came flying out the open door. The other one got caught by the half-closed window. I left Bessie and went into the house to help Clippy.

"Mrs. Patstegre, take Dr. Epy's right arm and I will take his left. Let's slice them off," Clippy said.

"No, Clippy. I think we have done enough. Besides, we have spent too much time here. I'm sure their gang is looking for them. Let's go home," I said.

"Okay, Mrs. Patstegre."

Clippy and I looked at each other. Our look wished that Dr. Epy and Norman would burn in hell for Amber, Ivan, and everyone who lost their life to fentanyl poisoning and fentanyl overdosing.

Clippy and I ran to Bessie. We jumped in and drove away.

The police would think that the attacks against Dr. Epy and Norman were gang related. There were several rival gangs living in Ladin that would take the credit.

Clippy and I were exhausted. It was the kind of tiredness that makes talking hard.

There was peace for now.

I drove Clippy home.

I woke up. I laid in bed thinking.
Could mind killing weaken fury? Maybe.

When would the world realize that mental illness was behind so much addiction and hopelessness? Maybe in my next life, God would send me, an advocating Caregiver, back down to earth, to change the broken mental health system.

State of the art hospitals, long term rehabilitation, and employment purpose paths were a must. Knowledge from Psychiatrists and Doctors of Care–Caregivers should be listened to. Tons of money was needed for the mentally ill.

I looked up.

"Talking Ceiling, my love as a Mother and Caregiver takes me down protective paths of slaying slugs that I'm convinced are evil. These mind wearing costumes that I create take on personalities that lead the way to releasing my wrath.

"Clippy, my best friend, and I are a team. We acted like Wyatt Earp and Bat Masterton wearing Marshal stars of justifiable violence in my mind killing dream.

"Talking Ceiling, is it bad to have these mind killing dreams? Is it bad not to tell Clippy that she is in my dreams?" I asked.

"Mrs. Patstegre, it is not bad. I believe your wrath is so strong that your nightmares seem real to you. I assume from what you say about Clippy, she wants justice as much as you do. That is why Clippy is in the mind kill dreams with you. Mind kills are private. I believe keeping the mind kills to yourself is for the best," Talking Ceiling answered.

"I'm sure you are right. Thank you," I said.

"Mrs. Patstegre, you are a good person doing your best to give chronic care in a world that fails the mentally ill.

Watching Speet suffer, empowers you to mind kill while you sleep. You mind kill to validate your anger and soothe your longing for justice. I understand things that you say and do," Talking Ceiling said.

"Talking Ceiling. Help me forget these free flying flights of fiction," I said.

"Okay, Mrs. Patstegre. Close your eyes and I will play music to filter out your concerns," Talking Ceiling said.

How was Talking Ceiling going to play music? I was too tired to ask.

I heard quiet rain outside. I heard soft, soothing guitar music that sounded familiar. I fell back to sleep in peace.

Diary Entry 24 - September 15

Happy Birthday to my grandmother. She was a great woman. She divorced her fun loving, drinking Irish husband to save her house and family. She sewed in a factory and made a complete life for herself and her girls. To divorce in the 1930's was Rosa Parks brave. Stigma was strong. Will power to go against the stigma was lioness.

Diary Entry 25 - September 16

Being tired from lack of sleep did not compare to being tired from being misunderstood.

Diary Entry 26 - September 18

"I see a stillness that will eventually kill me for no reason. Would God take me knowing the things I did or didn't do on Earth? Maybe. I have felt the fire of stigma, disgust, and stupidity. The ashes of hell will feel lukewarm to me in comparison to the fire I have felt here on earth," I said.

I took a breath. Ah, I forgot my sister, Effie, was in the room with me.

"You say things with such determined passion. I try to understand. I really do but I haven't been through what you have," Effie said.

"Effie, it is hard to find middle ground in caring. Some people dismiss Caregiving and the importance of it. People love to say it is not really a job if you aren't getting paid. They love to say that you're not a doctor. Oh, but we are. We are Doctors of Care.

"There are slow motion locomotives going down tracks to help mental illness. Why does positive change have to be slow? Change can go fast to outer space by the rich for their enjoyment and conceit.

"Change goes fast at our border with benefits. Benefits are also needed for the mentally ill, homeless, and people addicted to drugs. Change is slow for a cause unless an elite gets on the train, sees what the ride is like, and goes through several crashes.

"Do the elite ruling/political classes get platinum health and retirement plans? I would think that they do, but I could be wrong. If a loved one of theirs becomes mentally ill, their health plan super speeds care. Maybe that is one reason why mental illness reform is not at the top of the docket among politicians.

"Normal people pay for health care plans that have minimum coverage for those with mental illness. It's hard to find a psychiatrist that takes insurance and doesn't have a wait list. There is acute care when someone is in crisis. It is called intake where the patient stays at a hospital for a week or two. Acute care is not enough.

"Where is the St. Jude Philosophy for the mentally ill? Where are the long-term residential programs after acute care for a loved one suffering from a mental illness for the middle class and the poor? Residential long-term care should be covered by insurance and if not, it should be available to those in need for reasonable costs. Many suffering from mental illness survive with long-term care from Caregiving family members," I concluded.

Effie gleamed with her empathetic eyes and listening lips.

"I agree with what you said. I wish with all my heart that I could make it better," Effie said.

I hugged her.

"Writing at this moment is the best way that I may begin to defrost my inner core. Thanks for listening, Effie," I said.

Diary Entry 27 - September 19

Ode to Mr. Patstegre.

September 19 was an anniversary of a gentleman and a lady. We fell for each other. Youth and marriage brought us energy, speed, and Speet. Aging brought us energy with a pause and speed with some discomfort. Ten more years brought us energy with thought and speed with caution.

Call it 80-20, 70-30, 60-40, co-pays of affection, care, and giving in. The ratios could change depending on what was going on in our lives. The insurance policy of continuation was based on who at what time and what crisis would jump into action when they knew the other one couldn't.

It was knowing and accepting our agreed upon jobs, being good at our jobs, and knowing how to survive through grief, transitions, disputes, and medical crises, both mental and physical.

It was walking together with the same values. It was knowing when to appreciate and love the aging hands, aging body, aging hair, aging mind, and aging slowness.

We said for better or worse and stuck to it.

With aging, it was no longer the limber legs that jumped and ran without thinking. It was not the bottomless eating and still looking the same the next day. It was not the spending and not caring where it came from. It was not the endless days of school, sports, and parties.

"Mr. Patstegre, you went to Heaven before me. I will hold your hand in my hand and your heart in my heart for however long I am here on Earth," I whispered.

Diary Entry 28 - September 22

The hot water massaged my back and brain as I showered for the day. Fifteen minutes was my limit. I had to get to work by eight. I had a cleaning job at the Scans.

Half brick, half wood adorned the front of the Scan's house. Green year-round boxwoods lined the cracked concrete sidewalk that led to the front door.

The two older Scans had the same anatomy. They had two little boys, each one from different women. Lovely family. Daddy Bob, as I called him, bragged in a good way, about his family when I interviewed him on the phone.

I let myself in the front door. They left it open for me. The door creaked. It welcomed me in a high pitch scream, in anticipation of what I might do in the house. Doors were shields for the family to stand behind if necessary.

I looked around. I saw two boys. They looked about twelve and ten. I spoke with them for a couple of minutes while they prepared their backpacks for school. Their Dads appeared. They rushed to the car.

"Thanks in advance, Mrs. Patstegre, for the deep clean. Your check is on the counter," Daddy Sam said.

I waved good-bye.

In just five minutes, I noticed a few things about each boy. Each child favored their biological Dad's looks. The older son had a cautious blue-eyed stare and a me attitude toward life. The other son, dimple grinned and carried a white flag in his pocket. Both boys were good outwardly and knew their place with each other. It made it hard to do a mean cleaning instead of nice dusting.

I carried Minnet, Vacky and Shiffty to the second floor. I placed them on the floor.

The house was not dirty. The Scans had picked up things from the floor. There was little clutter. They made my deep cleaning job easy. As I made one of the beds, I looked out the window facing the backyard. I noticed a junkyard in the backyard.

I decided the junkyard-backyard needed me more than an interior cleaning of the Scan's house.

I looked outside. I noticed a sheepdog, a lab, a lassie style dog, and a toy poodle. The dogs were filthy.

The Scans lived in the country, far from their neighbors. The houses were so spread out that this large junkyard-backyard was seen only by the Scans.

After cleaning their house, I spent bewitching time in their backyard.

Minnet, my cleaning spray, oversaw scrubbing the dogs. Vacky, my vacuum, hosed the dogs down and chased them around the yard. The cycle continued until all were clean. I swore the eyes of the dogs said thank you.

I gathered many little pieces of wood with nails sticking out of them, old clothes, old ripped up books, magazines, and other discarded items. I found a large aluminum container that looked like one we used to burn leaves in when I was young. You know, the kind that had holes about three inches in diameter all over it and stood about five feet tall.

I threw junk in the aluminum container and torched it. Brilliant colors flamed. The flames swatted each other. What a nice sight, a step toward a better yard for everyone, purging by flame.

I felt the Scans would be thrilled. They were. Daddy Bob and Daddy Sam came home earlier than expected or I was there longer than anticipated. Daddy Bob and Daddy Sam thanked me.

"We work long days to make ends meet. The dogs and the junk accumulated. We love dogs. Time limits neglected their care; limited storage explains the junk. Thank you, Mrs. Patstegre. It looks great," Daddy Sam said.

I nodded. Niceness today. A softness surrounded me for the dogs that needed care.

Diary Entry 29 - September 23

I wondered how Speet was doing this morning. He alluded the other day that he wanted to attend graduate school, play music out at night, or do both. He sounded sincere. I'm sure we would talk more about it.

In the meantime, my typewriter fingers hit the right keys with the right fingers most of the day. My fingers moved to melodies of make believe.

Diary Entry 30 - September 25

Unfairness was the pre-existing condition to action. I had, I took, you didn't, you gave, were highlights of hidden feelings from trauma. I was fearful that no one was listening because nothing seemed to match the intensity of unfairness that I felt. It seemed the louder I talked, the less someone listened. Intensity was bad breath repelling.

I laid down on my bed. I was worn out from too much unresolved thinking. Would that unresolved thinking cause me to mind kill tonight?

I fell into a deep sleep.

I found myself drifting toward my phone. I called Clippy in my dream.

"Clippy, do you want to go out again tonight?" I asked.

Her answer was, "Hell, yes."

"Great, I will be over soon and we can talk about things," I said.

Clippy and I longed for justice. We were Caregivers. We were connected.

It was time to pick up Clippy. I arrived at her house.

"Bessie, toot-toot to get Clippy out here. Not too loud," I said.

"Okay, Mrs. Patstegre," Bessie said.

Bessie whispered a toot-toot.

Clippy ran down the steep hill in front of her house. She climbed into the passenger side of Bessie.

She had black tight leggings on her skinny legs. She wore a matching black top that barely covered her stomach. Her clothes were a stark contrast to her barbie doll face, hair, and complexion. Vanity was a trait of this tattooed eyeliner, girl friend of mine.

"How many times have I asked you to wear a longer shirt. After all, we can't have our victims attracted to us, can we?" I asked.

"Ha Ha, Mrs. Patstegre. Bad people need killing. The less clothes I have on, the less victim's blood I will have to wash off later," Clippy answered.

I smiled at Clippy.

"Mrs. Patstegre, where are we going tonight?" Clippy asked.

"I'll tell you on the way," I said.

Bessie hooted with delight. Bessie's spark plugs felt a flight of fairness coming. Her battery energized her.

Bessie hugged Clippy and me with her feel-good music of "Baby, I need your loving." Bessie bumped us up and down on the road. Her insides creaked and squeaked from age.

Oh, her accelerator! She soared to sixty miles an hour, faster than a hummingbird flies. I loved Bessie. It was hard for people to understand that she seemed human to me. I couldn't imagine my life without her beige welcoming exterior and her worn interior.

"Clippy, we are off to the south side of Fort Lace, about fifteen minutes away. Fort Lace has a Farmers' Market on Fridays. I have an idea. I need you to trust me," I said.

"You are the boss, Mrs. Patstegre. Whatever you decide, I am okay with," Clippy said.

"When we get there, we will stomp and smash. Skin color does not matter. Tattoos don't matter. Rich or poor does not matter. Vigilante motives will take place tonight guided by my keen frontal lobes of organization and my amygdala emotions," I said.

"Oh, Mrs. Patstegre, I love when you talk. I say let's mess up someone evil. I have anger like you. Where do we find our vile asshole, Mrs. Patstegre?" Clippy asked.

"You will soon find out," I answered.

Every Friday there was a Farmers' Market during the day on 9th Street. The booths closed at six o'clock at night. In an alley behind 9th Street, the farmers and people running the booths, disposed of the fruit and vegetables that could not be given away.

We drove down the alley that ran parallel and behind 9th Street. It was dark. Chipped red bricks on the lower parts of the buildings lined the alley along the ground. Rats ran from garbage pile to garbage pile. Broken streetlights holding just bulbs and a few pieces of jagged glass lit the alley. Bessie dimmed her wide-eyed headlights. She put her auburn, rectangular parking lights on instead.

"Clippy, I brought two pairs of heavy-duty boots for us to stomp in, the kind with bottoms that could scar for a lifetime. Could you please grab them from the back seat of Bessie?" I asked.

"Sure thing," Clippy answered.

We put the boots on. The deep crevasses on the soles would leave marks of destruction behind.

"Clippy, you watch, I do. I watch, you do. You learn, I stomp. I learn, you stomp. You cheer, I jump. I cheer, you jump. We're going to stomp these boots of fairness until things are penny flat," I said.

We got out of Bessie. I had my ripped up blue jean jacket on. It was so worn that one of the arms, if tugged, would fall off at the elbow. We both wore black baseball caps.

We walked around the puddles in the alley. We traveled down the passageway hoping to find the target before time narrowed.

"Clippy, take my hand and I will show you a safe way of releasing our displeasure and discontent," I said.

Clippy cocked her head and squinted at me. I knew she did not quite understand what I meant. Clippy toughed her mouth with hard ass words giving the impression she could handle anything. I knew better. She was fragile at times. I thought she needed to slow down.

In front of us was a big dumpster that held most of the rotten fruit and vegetables that couldn't be sold or given away. Around the perimeter of the dumpster were watermelons and cantaloupes that didn't make it into the dumpster.

"Clippy, do you see all the rotten watermelons and cantaloupes on the ground?" I asked.

"I sure do, Mrs. Patstegre," Clippy answered.

"Clippy, I want you to close your eyes while we stomp on this fruit. I want you to think of our veterans and people who have had severe trauma. They suffer from Post-Traumatic Stress Disorder – PTSD. Discrimination and the misinterpretation of their rageful and restless symptoms are witnessed everyday against the people we love and know that suffer from PTSD. I want you to think of the destruction, death, and trauma that our Veterans and trauma victims live with.

"Crush the visions of killing that Veterans have seen and have done. Squash the nightmares that live with trauma victims. As you trample on the melons, think the fruit are horrible symptoms of mental illness that victims carry such as cratered depression, volcanic mania, "roadrunner" anxiety, rollercoaster fear, panic and paranoia, and feeling unsafe.

"Clippy, flatten the stigmatic shameful tongues spreading untruths about our Veterans and all that suffer from PTSD. Stomp and squash the intense anxiety, stress, fear, rage, and nightmares that they walk and talk with every day," I concluded.

"Okay, Mrs. Patstegre, let's stomp and crush," Clippy said.

"We have car lifting strength. Trample the cruel treatment that force Veterans to the streets and unemployment lines," I said.

Tired and drained, we finished the crushing fruit ceremony. We walked to Bessie.

We rinsed off with gallon sized jugs of water I had in the back of Bessie. We changed our clothes and bagged up our mess.

"Clippy, I hope you are not too disappointed. I felt we needed to calm down our intensity," I said.

"I'm not disappointed. I love you," Clippy said.

We drove home in a state of exhausted fogginess and clear fairness. The melon stomping adventure was a successful and harmless release.

"Goodnight, Clippy."

Clippy held her aching back, slid down the front seat of Bessie until her feet touched the ground. She walked up the hill to her front porch. She turned, waved, and went inside.

I woke up in my bed. My mind killing dream was over.

"Talking Ceiling, are you there?" I asked.

"Yes, I'm here," Talking Ceiling said.

"Talking Ceiling, you are the only one that knows about my mind kills. Clippy is my partner in these mind kills. She knows nothing of these fictional escapes. I wish I could tell her about them. I know you think that's a bad idea because you think these mind killing dreams will show me the way to deal with my buried sadness and grief.

"Tonight, however, I had a different, less potent, nightmare. My torment may be starting to walk a plank of feeling so that someday I might plunge into a sea of seeing and sorrow," I said.

"Mrs. Patstegre, I would be happy if you started to feel deep emotions just a little bit. I believe, setting free these emotions will guide you to take better care of yourself," Talking Ceiling said.

"You know, Talking Ceiling, you are smart. I will get there, sooner than later, I hope. My irritating intensity surges into a high wave and can stay there during a mind kill. I long for a lower wave to ride in the future," I said.

"Mrs. Patstegre, please close your eyes. Give me your thoughts and I will put them on your bookshelf. Go back to sleep," Talking Ceiling said.

"Thank you, Talking Ceiling."

I did what she said. I drifted back to sleep, to peaceful thoughts.

Diary Entry 31 - October 3

Vacky the vacuum, Shiffty the mop, and Minnet the cleaning spray were awake in the pantry closet. They usually stayed in the closet until I needed them. Today was different.

Vacky, Shiffty, and Minnet did not hear me in the kitchen. I usually woke up at six o'clock in the morning. They suspected something was wrong. Vacky's handle pushed open the door. Off the trio went. Vacky led the way to the oak stairs. Vacky, Shiffty, and then Minnet hopped in synch on different stairs until they jumped into my bedroom.

"Mrs. Patstegre, we were worried about you. It's nine in the morning, three hours after you rise," said Vacky, Shiffty, and Minnet.

I sat up. I pushed my hair out of my face.

"Thanks for caring. I slept in. I was thought tired," I said.

"What do you mean?" Vacky chimed in on an A note.

"What do you mean?" Shiffty chimed in on a B note.

"What do you mean?" Minnet chimed in on a C note.

"Vacky, Shiffty, and Minnet, I am responsible for sandpapering the edges to tones and words. I am responsible for seeing that Speet has food and necessities. I am responsible for asking the best questions for care. I am responsible for fine tuning my reflective everything skills.

"I get scared of my physical limitations as the aging process takes hold. My hands of octagon descent have carried heavy weights. I have worn down veins, arteries, muscles, tendons, organs, brains cells, hormones, and neurotransmitters," I said.

The trio sighed and came closer. Vacky's upper handle hugged me. Shiffty stood on her handle and shook away my fears. Minnet sprayed and cleaned with her little white gloved hands to make me feel good.

"Thank you, my friends. Aging physically and mentally makes you think of pulling others into your Caregiving Circle. The Caregiver's knowledge and intuition is unique to their experiences and learned habits. This knowledge can be taught to others that have the Caregiving calling," I said.

I looked at my big-hearted friends, Vacky, Shiffty, and Minnet.

"Now hop back downstairs," I said.

"Come on troops. Follow me down in the same way that we hopped up," Vacky said.

Summa Cum Laude Caretakers demanded answers.

"Ritalin the grants, government, and corporations to move faster and focus on mental health," I said to myself as I stepped on the floor of another day.

Diary Entry 32 - October 5

People loved to tell me to take more time for myself. If I didn't then I was being lazy or not making myself a priority. When did Caregivers, given a choice, make themselves the priority? When were Caregivers lazy?

Something or someone needed to nudge self-care. In my case, aging and the increasing and nagging physical limitations, prompted me to at least acknowledge that the coming of age was upon me.

Diary Entry 33 - October 14

Many people were narcissists. Their sensitivity and vainness revolved inside of them. Their lack of compassion and knowledge spun outside of them.

Why did narcissists think that someone experiencing symptoms of irritability from a mental illness, threw their harsh words/moods at them? Why did narcissists take them to heart? When were symptoms of any disease aimed at anyone except the person themselves suffering from the illness?

Shame slumped shoulders, childlike attraction to idealism, and the need for safety and gentleness became the norm after Speet got triggered. His symptoms waterfalled out in all directions. Speet experienced many narcissists judging him.

This was when I screamed, "Don't condemn me, a Caregiver, for my mind killing thoughts. My love provides unstoppable protection for my loved ones. I will always find a way to help them, always."

Diary Entry 34 - October 15

I tossed and turned as I tried to sleep. The turmoil stopped.

I fell into a deep sleep. I started dreaming.

I found myself floating toward the wolves and crows who were calling me.

The howls and the cackles energized me to call Clippy in my dream.

"Clippy, I know you hear the wolves howl like I do. Tonight, could be another night that we make a difference. Are you in?" I asked.

"Mrs. Patstegre, I'm all in," Clippy said.

"Bessie and I will be over soon," I said.

I was pepper mad, might have grown a tail, and was red in desire to costume cape my way around town.

Honesty lined my cloak of spreading awareness. Getting rid of stigma and discrimination seamed through my clothes.

I knew someone Clippy and I could tackle. His name was Flip Flynn. He was a journalist. He wrote many articles for a local newspaper. He slandered mental illness with stigmatic rhetoric.

Reading his articles over the past years boiled my blood. I envisioned spilling his blood for all the nonsense and misinformation that he printed in his anti-mental health articles.

Flip Flynn's remarks attributed crime and violence to the mentally ill. He used the word "crazy" as a nickname to describe people who suffered from mental illnesses in his writings.

Flip Flynn wrote in an article, "All people who are mentally ill are violent." That kind of reporting produced a false perception that all people suffering from mental illness were responsible for the violence in life. One article questioned the character of someone mentally ill, as if they chose to have symptoms such as irritability, restlessness, panic, irrational thoughts, and desperation.

Pain from the disease of mental illness caused symptoms just like the pain from cancer and its treatment caused symptoms. Pain was pain. Why was physical pain accepted and mental pain jailed?

Another negative article written by Flip Flynn said, "Having mental health problems are a sign of weakness. These people can't be productive in society."

Flip Flynn's misinformation sent messages to those who suffered to delay treatment. False information forced people suffering from mental illness to hide their disease instead of developing coping skills. His articles caused low self-esteem to flourish.

I wrote numerous letters to Flip Flynn expressing my advocate views on his incorrect words. His lack of response solidified my hound dog intuition that Flip Flynn didn't care. He wasn't going to change his damaging thinking.

I wanted a cosmopolitan of surprise, spontaneity, and sizzle for Flip Flynn. After all, mental illness surprised people. It picked them, not the other way around. Mental Illness could hit and tackle anyone, not just someone genetically vulnerable.

My thoughts urged action. I hopped into Bessie. I turned on music using her old-fashioned CD player. "Stairway to Heaven" came on. Speet must have put a Led Zeppelin CD in when he borrowed my car. I sped just fast enough not to get a ticket. Bessie's worn leather seats wrinkled with age. She meant more to me now than when I first bought her.

I flashed Bessie's lights at Clippy's house. She ran down her steep front yard.

"The grass is so wet. I almost fell. I'm excited for tonight, Mrs. Patstegre," Clippy said.

"Clippy, let's use the power of our care and advocacy to rid the unfairness that birthed mental illness and ghost picked our loved ones to invade. We must seek truth for all those suffering. Our vampire bites will suck out evil. Our actions will spread awareness and decrease stigma," I said.

"I agree. Here's my way of saying what I think you just said. Let's go slap around someone spreading untruths." Clippy said.

Clippy had her tight black leggings on. They tandemed nicely with her skinny legs. This was a staple in her wardrobe. She wore a black oversized sweatshirt, a switch from her usual short tops.

"Where to Mrs. Patstegre?" Clippy asked.

"We are going to Flip Flynn's house. He is a journalist. He writes untrue articles about mental illness. We need to remedy that," I said.

I knew where he lived. Our hands of harm and our hearts of love were our fuel, our electricity that ignited our night.

"We are here, Clippy," I said.

Clippy's large feet had glow in the dark white shoes on. They lit up our pathway.

We tiptoed into the backyard of a tainted and untruthful journalist. Tree frogs and crickets were chirping to each other, wishing us success. The water in the pool was crystal clear like our mission.

Maybe we would collide with this pool of perfect dimensions later.

The sliding glass doors in the back of the house were open. There were not any security cameras. Lucky for us, unlucky for pompous, hurtful journalist, Flip Flynn.

We slid the fingerprint free sliding doors open enough to enter. No pictures of kids anywhere. Good, no kids. We saw a guy sleeping, snoring, middle aged, maybe divorced, maybe not, and alone. We checked the other two rooms. No one else was here.

"Well, Flip Flynn, Clippy and I are here. We can be your guests for a while. It's time for you to get tongue-tied from spreading false statements. You need to start researching, listening, and telling the truth," I whispered.

We had gloves on and old-fashioned babushkas. Our sixty plus-year-old bodies complemented our hundred-year-old minds. My heart rate and blood pressure were lower than normal.

Calm was coming. Fairness was coming. Love and peace were coming.

"Follow my lead, Clippy. Here is a regular somewhat sharp kitchen knife. I have a similar one," I said.

We jumped like cougars pouncing on the fortyish faceless male.

Clippy's karate hands attacked first. We slashed, four, five, thirteen times for the stigma Flip Flynn encouraged with his untruths. It looked like Clippy wanted to do more. Should we?

"Wait a minute, Clippy. Stop. Flip Flynn looks like he might be in shock. He isn't moving much," I said.

The blood of this liar was dripping from his knife wounds. None of his slashes were deep.

"Clippy, we can accomplish more by letting Flip Flynn live. We can encourage him to write articles of awareness and advocacy for mental illness, thereby decreasing stigma," I said.

"How would we get him to do that, Mrs. Patstegre?" Clippy asked.

"I'm not sure. Something inside is telling me to stop slashing Flip Flynn – to stop his blood from splattering on the walls, creating a painting of dots and dashes. He deserves us to continue like a pack of wolves and rip him apart. Yet, we might achieve more to convince Flynn to alter his beliefs and print true facts about mental illness," I answered.

"Well, okay, Mrs. Patstegre," Clippy said.

We sat Flip Flynn up. His wounds were minor. We splashed water on his face. He became attentive. Clippy and I explained in detail how his stories of lies hurt the mentally ill, Caregivers, and anyone else in the circle of care.

Flip Flynn held a towel on his wounds. The three of us walked to the pool and sat down to talk. It didn't hurt that Clippy and I still had the knives in our hands. We might have alluded once or thirteen times, to the fact that we would haunt him if his hurtful journalist mind, heart, and hands didn't print compassionate and accurate statements about the stigma and cruelness that exists in the world toward the mentally ill.

We wanted him to bring truth to many who are unaware of what people suffering from mental illness go through. Writing correct facts about symptoms of mental illness would decrease the stigma associated with those symptoms.

Flip Flynn faded away from the pool as Clippy and I walked away.

As we drove home, I looked at Clippy.

"Are you okay?" I asked.

"I'm good," Clippy answered.

"Clippy, tonight, we weaponized our minds and beat Flynn with words of truth rather than knife wounds. We conquered and overpowered a pig who was squealing untruths.

"Watch out gossip and false statements. We are supporters of honest facts. We battle for empathy and kindness. Don't use harmful rhetoric around us. We will correct every untruth. Right, Clippy," I said.

I looked at Clippy. Her head bobbed in a freaky freedom dance. I laughed. We triumphed.

Our conquest spirited us home. Flynn, the fake reporter, got flipped into going a better direction with his writing. He promised us that he would no longer spread false statements about the mentally ill. We baptized him into clarity. He was a reborn pup going to bark fair reporting about the lives of the mentally ill and the lives of Caregivers.

I smiled at Clippy. She smiled at me.

"Goodbye, dear friend," I said.

"Goodbye, Mrs. Patstegre." Clippy said.

I sat up in my bed and yawned. My mind kill dream was over.

Right after a mind kill dream, I was sure my vigilante deeds happened. I didn't care if that pinpoint of doubt wanted to stick me at times. I wouldn't believe the sting. I believed the vision. It helped me cope. Words and actions of horror were imagined by me to anger-reveal what the thief named mental illness stole from loved ones.

If I revealed my mind killing dreams to anyone, any therapist, or any psychiatrist, what would they think? Should I care? My diary didn't care. It opened whenever words needed to release rawness.

If anyone cared for and watched the wretchedness of mental illness, they would understand my need to let out distasteful words and actions that hugged my inner pain. Life wasn't the same when mental illness encircled a loved one.

"Talking Ceiling, are you awake?" I asked.

"Always, for you, Mrs. Patstegre," Talking Ceiling answered.

"Talking Ceiling, my mind kills have allowed deep torment and worry to surface. Including Clippy in my mind kills helps me act out her grief even though our conversations and actions are not real. I wish I could tell Clippy about them but I can't. The mind kills are visualized for my recovery and mine alone.

"The mind killing of Flip Flynn turned out differently than I thought. I wonder why?" I said.

"Mrs. Patstegre. Maybe your inner desire to take better care of yourself wants to carve a place for comfort and peace in your life. Maybe you wish to tone down your angry thoughts," Talking Ceiling said.

"You may be right, Talking Ceiling. For now, I think my laundry is calling me to rumble it into the dryer. I will be back shortly," I said.

"Okay, Mrs. Patstegre. Watch a good detective show. I know how much you like these shows, especially the ones that involve forensic details. Do you think you might be able to go back sleep?" Talking Ceiling asked.

"I'm not sure, Talking Ceiling," I answered.

Diary Entry 35 - October 16

I never did go back to bed after my mind killing dream last night. I managed to do a couple batches of laundry.

It was about six in the morning. I opened the back door and sat on the steps. It was quiet. The sky was untroubled. I sat and mindfully took in the presence of a new day. It felt good.

Diary Entry 36 - October 17

"Talking Ceiling are you there?" I asked.

"I am, Mrs. Patstegre. How can I help you?"

"I'm tired tonight so I hope I will be able to sleep well. To help me relax, can you please play that sweet music that you played for me before?" I asked.

"Yes, I can, Mrs. Patstegre. Close your eyes and rest," Talking Ceiling answered.

"Thank you, Talking Ceiling," Mrs. Patstegre said.

"I will make time for you whenever you want," Talking Ceiling said.

My eyes twinkled. They shut. I heard soft mandolin and guitar music. The music soothed me. I fell asleep.

Diary Entry 37 - October 19

It rained hard on my bedroom windows. I rolled snail-like out of bed. I took a quick shower. I wore jeans, a black sweater, and cowboy boots. I buckled myself in and drove off to Concerned Care Nursing Home.

It continued raining as I drove. I parked at Concerned Care. I grabbed my purse and goodies for my Lovelies. Lovelies was the name I decided to call the wonderful people I cared for at Concerned Care.

I ran to the front doors of the nursing home. I felt drops of pleasantry all over.

The soft and hard raindrops leeched feelings out of me. I had no power to stop the rain. It was an itsy-bitsy chance to feel, see, smell, hear, and taste. I loved it. I needed it.

I saw the straightness of rain. I smelt the rawness of the grass. I circled around with my eyes closed. I heard ping pong rain bouncing off the bricks and concrete. My imagination tasted the food the rain grew. The rain hypnotized me. This trance led me down a well of momentary feelings.

I shook the rain off me.

"Hi Crystal. How is school?" I asked.

"It's great. The work is hard but I love it. I'm hanging in there," Crystal answered.

"I'm happy things are working out for you. I better run and set up my Care-Cart," I said.

I bought small pumpkins for Halloween for everyone that I cared for. I also brought my usual magazines and newspapers. I added *USA Today* to my newspaper supply.

I scooted to the room where my Care-Cart was. I loaded up my cart. I saw two nurses on my floor. They gave me medical snacks for my cart. I wheeled on.

As I grabbed a couple of magazines for a ninety-year-old man, someone jogged by me. I caught a quick click of a view. Instinct thought I knew him. He dipped sideways into the door leading to the steps at the end of the hall and was gone. Oh well.

I knocked on Ms. File's door. Some doors had sweet wreaths with sentimental items on them. Ms. File had nothing. A plain white, simple door greeted me.

"Come in," Ms. File said.

"It's you, Mrs. Patstegre. I missed you. Is everything okay?" Ms. File asked.

"Yes, everything is fine," I answered.

I thought to myself, no it wasn't. I mind killed or hurt bad people in my dreams.

"Oh, Ms. File, you painted a new rose painting. You capture true color. Your paint brush has realism on one side and impressionism on the other. Your colorful roses speak to me.

"You painted young, smooth, and fresh roses. I dried roses the other day. The dried roses revealed new versions of the original roses. Both roses show beauty. A two in one rose exists in everyone," I said.

"Mrs. Patstegre, I appreciate that you like and get inspired by my paintings. Painting makes me happy. It gives purpose to my day," Ms. File said.

"You are a woman of many talents, Ms. File," I said.

Ms. File coughed. Her cough barked in a biting way. I didn't like it. I thought she looked thinner.

"Are you okay, Ms. File. Should I call a nurse?" I asked.

Ms. File caught her breath. She stopped coughing.

"No thanks, Mrs. Patstegre. I'm sure it is a side effect to a new medicine that I am taking," Ms. File answered.

"I have your approved snack. I also have your *Wall Street Journal* and *New York Times*. How about a *People* magazine for fun?" I asked.

"Sure, I will take a *People* magazine, Mrs. Patstegre," Ms. File answered.

"Here is a small pumpkin for Halloween. I hope it recites stories about Halloween. Imagination conquers loneliness," I said with a smile.

I grew fond of Ms. File. The deepness in her eyes intrigued me. In the future, I would leave her room until last. I wanted to spend more time conversing with her.

"Thanks for the pumpkin. See you next time," said Ms. File.

"See you soon, Ms. File. Oh, I almost forgot. Here is a quote from History. 'There can be no deep disappointment where there is no deep love,'" I said.

"Hmmm, don't tell me. Let me think. Is it Martin Luther King?" Ms. File asked.

"Yes, it is," I answered.

I waved good-bye.

Now to Mr. Gaudan's room.

"Good morning. I'm Mrs. Patstegre. I am the Care-Cart Lady. You might not remember me. I met you last time I was here," I said.

Mr. Gaudan looked up at me. His Oreo colored hair stuck up a tad.

"I remember you. You are the newspaper lady. Right?" Mr. Gaudan asked.

"Yes, I am. I have newspapers, magazines, pens, paper, etc. I have an approved snack for you. I also brought you a real pumpkin for Halloween," I said.

"Great. I will take a *Wall Street Journal* like last time. That's it. Good-bye. Close the door when you leave," Mr. Gaudan said.

I contemplated doing what gruff Mr. Gaudan wanted. Instead, I didn't take his gruff words to heart - DTTH.

"Mr. Gaudan, I listened to you last time I was here. I reminded myself when I saw you again, to tell you that I agree with your insight into the lack of care given from children to aging parents. After all, we cared for them through their awkward, stubby, and stubborn years. Did we deport them to teenage camp permanently? No," I said.

Mr. Gaudan looked up with gentle eyes.

"You did listen to me. I'm grateful," Mr. Gaudan said.

"Children pedal their parents around and so many drop them off at Nursing Homes. Shut all the lips of children burping out the burden word at their seventy and eighty-years-old parents. No one aborted them and shot their pre-existence to hell.

"Ungratefulness is the escalator that kills us early. Living in a box for a room coffins us right into God's hands.

"Pardon me, Mr. Gaudan. I don't know you that well. I got carried away. I'm sorry," I said.

Mr. Gaudan gazed at me.

"I'm thankful for your kind words. I may not be somebody to my kids; I'm somebody to you," Mr. Gaudan said.

"Oh, my. I can get used to your complements, Mr. Gaudan. You had good reasons to be gruff during our talk last time I was here. Discardment, is that a word? Oh, well.

"Discardment done by loved ones is despicable. Helping hands should grab hold of the worn, wise, and wonderful Caregivers that the elderly once were. Children, loved ones, and other family members should take care of older family members willingly," I said.

"When are you coming back?" Mr. Gaudan asked.

"When you comb your hair, ha-ha. Take care," I answered.

I ran to Bessie. It was late. Speet and I scheduled a dinner tonight to talk about him going back to school. I hoped that our talk would go well.

When I got home, Speet asked if we could talk tomorrow.

I nodded and agreed.

Diary Entry 38 - October 20

Sleep was necessary and unnecessary. Since it was three o'clock in the morning, this was a morning of unnecessary sleep. So, I worked. I read.

Laundry churned in the background.

I wondered if other Caregivers were up.

I stood up.

"How many Caregivers write fictional diaries with tornadoes of truth in it? Can my words parallel other Caregivers' thoughts? Can I connect the dots of Caregivers into a picture of sameness? Yes, I can. So many of us. So much love. So much care. So much courage," I said out loud.

I wanted to get some sleep. I laid down in my bed.

Later today, Speet and I were going to talk about him going to school. I wanted to be able to focus and help him. I closed my eyes. Talking Ceiling had other thoughts.

"So, Mrs. Patstegre, how do you relieve your stress, worry, and anger?" Talking Ceiling asked.

"I mind kill people that cast aside goodness. These duty deed mind kills scream vulgarity and vomit. They allow me to talk decently and live with dignity. You know this Talking Ceiling," I answered.

"Mrs. Patstegre, Caregivers like you suffer from high anxiety, little sleep, and lack of care for themselves. You deal with high-grade suffering that is too deep for you to see and feel. Hopeful windows for relief are often not opened for you or by you. Mrs. Patstegre, I watch you go through your day in a low-grade sadness. No one else can see this. I can," Talking Ceiling said.

"Well, Talking Ceiling, I don't want to deal with any of that, not quite yet. I make split second decisions. I use keen intuition grown from experience, beyond what Caregivers already have. Besides thinking what shoe is going to fall off and walking on eggshells, I sniff clues and memorize mannerisms for answers from loved ones. Right now, I'm a Centered Caregiver. I am good at hide and *see,*" I said.

"I don't want to hurt you. I want to help you, Mrs. Patstegre. You have rare and real feelings buried in you. Your uniqueness needs to touch the sunlight to come out," Talking Ceiling said.

"Why, Talking Ceiling, my word technique is wearing off on you. Mr. Patstegre tried a couple of times to compile words that sounded like me. I kindly reminded him that everyone has their own remarkable style of word communication.

"Right now, I am boiling Jell-O that needs to cool but I don't know when that will be. I am not ready to flood myself with cool and sad sensations. When I am, I will control the speed of that outpouring," I said.

Talking Ceiling kept me up for a while.

I finally fell asleep for a couple of hours.

I needed coffee when I woke. I made it weak so I could conquer many cups during the day.

I heard Speet. It was nine o'clock in the morning.
He hopped down the stairs liked he was on a pogo stick. He jumped to the floor from the third step. Kaboom! I ran toward the stairs.

"Just had to jump, Mom. I'm fine," Speet said.

"Glad you are okay. The noise scared me," I said.

Speet saw the coffee. He grabbed his favorite mug.

"I like your diluted coffee. I'm getting used to it, Mom," Speet said.

Speet sat at the counter.

"I thought about going to school to learn business skills. I can't see myself doing all that studying. Learning and playing music would be better for me. I can see myself getting a Master of Music and/or playing music out at night," Speet said.

"I invested money in stocks. I can sell some. You can use the money for tuition and play music at night. Books and work. Would that be a stretch for you?" I asked.

"Only one way to find out. I need to do it," Speet answered.

"Let me think about it," I said.

"Okay, Mom? I'm going to play my guitar now. Love you."

"Love you, too," I said.

Speet parachuted from his trauma after he came home. It took over ten years, but he landed on his feet most days. Would he leave home and be able to do the same?

I swallowed the last of the coffee. I ran upstairs, showered, pretended I was Cinderella, and put on a ball gown and glass slippers.

I fluttered my eyes, enough to see my jeans and cowboy boots, which were really what I had on.

The cowboy boots were appropriate. I planned on kicking questions up in the air at Gus and seeing how he caught them.

I cooked spaghetti for everyone at Hookum. I also planned on bringing salad, bread, and homemade snickerdoodle cookies to the soup kitchen.

Gus's oddity irked me. I intended to find out more about his game today.

When I arrived at Hookum, I started setting up. I soon found myself face to face, eye to eye, with Gus.

"Mrs. Patstegre, why do you do what you do? You feed the poor and give them your heart and time. You make sure they eat a good meal. You feed me small bits of information about you. You don't care if I get you or not," Gus said.

Gus seemed too interested in who I was. I was a private person. Why did he ask me so many questions? I wanted to figure out why Gus was here. What was he up to volunteering at Hookum?

He wanted to get to know me. He didn't have that kind of time; I was complicated. Complication shadowed me every day. Complication wanted to learn from me.

"While the pasta is heating up, Gus, why don't you put the salad into these bowls, and I will tell you a few things about why I do the things that I do," I said.

I gave him brief answers to everything he asked. I didn't trust him. I needed to *Mouse Trap* him. I strategized the level of *Risk* I took with him. *Concentration* was played to memorize and figure out what Gus's language was saying.

Diary Entry 39 - October 30

Tears were good to release if they were from a sad movie and had nothing to do with me. Goblins that flew around trying to scare tears of reality out of me didn't work.

Intensity and perseverance made me into the best Caregiver I could be. I needed and used…Mohammed Ali's confidence, Madame Curie's brains and devotion, and Mother Teresa's unconditional love and compassion. Three in one.

The familiar phrase for schools, companies, and the government of diversity, equity, and inclusion, appeared to wear blinders for the mentally ill and homeless.

Diary Entry 40 - November 8

A friend of mine felt compelled to inquire about my lack of socializing. She knew I was an extrovert; I got energized by people. She was curious why I stayed home most nights.

I explained to her that acquaintances' lives were not very important to me. This was harsh. In my Caregiving world, when I had a free moment, true friendship and love won over acquaintances.

Acquaintances were tongues of shallow water people who waded around and quacked to see who got noticed the quickest.

"Oh, quack, I haven't eaten for a week; don't I look great? Especially to you size six fatties over there," a quack acquaintance said.

Thinness grabbed most of the attention, like the popular people in high school. Jealously existed in all of us, including me.

Then there were the men acquaintances quacking over each other to see who got heard the most. It was usually the one with the most money and perceived social standing. What did social standing mean anyway? Did those people with social standing not sit at parties? Did they stand on toilets, went poo poo fizz fizz, and sang "oh what a relief it is" when they went to the bathroom?

"Does that help?" I asked this friend who I now considered an acquaintance.

Diary Entry 41 - November 9

I, Mrs. Patstegre, a Caregiver, a Cleaner, a Cook, and a Mind Killer, were not separate personalities. I was one lady aware of her characteristics, jobs, and walks in life.

Diary Entry 42 - November 10

Rage, like morphine, was an analgesic that helped my sad pain stay quiet. It became my hit man. It was deadly. Lack of control coupled with a lack of power unleashed the best and the worst in me.

My temper puked out triggers. Trigger temper was noticeable. Silent temper was unnoticeable. Both were defense mechanisms for unresolved emotions.

I was convinced my rage would last a lifetime. I hoped I was wrong.

Diary Entry 43 - November 23

My reputation for cleaning had spread. Mr. and Mrs. Mantes were interested in hiring me. They wanted to meet me in person. Why?

I found out why when I showed up at their house at around eight o'clock in the evening.

Mr. Mantes wore a red plaid blazer. His hairless head shone like egg whites cooked on a pie and the tassels on his loafers flipped back and forth when he walked. His handshake upon introduction was limp.

Mrs. Mantes also shook my hand. Instead of her eyes looking into mine, they glanced up and down my no make-up, blue jean self. Mrs. Mantes didn't smile much due to the tightness of her face. If actresses couldn't get face lifts right, what made the non-famous think they could. It was a shame.

If Mrs. Mantes had kept her brown, straight, shoulder length hair instead of perming it, left her face alone, and thrown a down to earth jacket on instead of her short fur coat, she would still have turned heads.

The Mantes offered twice as much money than what I normally charged to clean, trying to entice me to clean for them on a regular schedule.

"I deep clean once. This is how I run my cleaning service," I said.

"Please, Mrs. Patstegre. Name your price. We really need someone every week. It is hard to find someone like you. You have a great reputation. I don't have the time to clean. Please, name your price," Mrs. Mantes said.

"Mrs. Mantes, my business consists of doing a deep clean on your house. I do not come back. When I am finished, your house will be in good order. I promise," I said.

"Well, I never. Who turns down a-name-your-price offer for cleaning? Don't you do this for the money? What is wrong with you?" Mrs. Mantes asked.

Mr. and Mrs. Mantes didn't deserve to know that I focused on the clean to avoid focusing on the un-clean pain of loss. That was my secret reason for cleaning that only I knew. I liked to clean when I wanted to and pick the clients on my terms. They didn't need to know any of my reasons for cleaning.

"What is wrong with me is that I agreed to meet you in person. Most people grab whatever date I have open over the phone. I should have guessed you had ulterior motives," I answered.

I walked toward the door. I reached for the doorknob, turned it, and that's when I heard words from Mr. Mantes.

"My dear Mrs. Mantes don't worry; we will find someone else. Anyway, I heard through the grapevine that Mrs. Patstegre enables her son, um I forget his name, by letting him live at home. You would think she would jump at the money," Mr. Mantes said.

At that moment, I wished I was amid a mind killing dream. I wasn't. I took deep breaths. I closed the door. I did not speed home. I would write. Yes, write.

I thanked Bessie for always being there for me, parked her in the garage, turned her off, blew her a kiss, and let myself into the house.

I threw my keys in a wooden box on my desk. They made a loud noise as they landed into the box. Vacky, Shiffty, and Minnet came out of the pantry closet located near my desk.

"Mrs. Patstegre, are you okay? You never throw your keys like that. Did someone hurt you? What can we do to help?" Vacky asked.

"Nothing, dear Vacky. Thank you for caring, you wonderful trio. I am going to listen to some music. I will let you know if I need anything," I answered.

"Mrs. Patstegre, we are here for you," Vacky spoke for all of them.

Vacky, Shiffty, and Minnet hopped back to the pantry. I went upstairs. I said good night to Speet.

I laid in bed, still clothed, closed my eyes, and prayed for peace so I could sleep, mind kill free.

Diary Entry 44 - November 28

I woke up early. I wrote the following motivational anagram on enabling. It was spurred on by my meeting with the Mantes.

_E_nergy for the Caregiver being called an enabler.

_N_eed to sew up loose lips spitting out false facts.

_A_dvocate against stigma.

_B_umbling idiots force us to be belligerent.

_L_azy minds that would rather remain ignorant than educate themselves. People need to become more educated about mental illness and listen to experienced Caregivers, mental health therapists, and psychiatrists about people that suffer from mental illness.

_I_njustice.

*N*eed to spark change.

*G*o silence the enabling word users. Caregivers try to figure-skate into a routine. We know how hard the ice feels in a crisis, a fall. We always get up. We support our loved ones to get up and stay up. We know when our loved ones can't do something. We will not shrink when we get old. Look for all the walking tall Caregivers in their sixties, seventies, eighties, and nineties.

Caregiving was in no way enabling. Anyone that said the word enabler in front of me, from now on, would get a mouth full of correction.

After meeting with Mr. and Mrs. Mantes, beside writing my enabler anagram, I envisioned and set free the following story.

Mr. Mantes was at a restaurant, telling exaggerated tales, and eating dinner with his wife and friends. In the middle of a boastful speech, he stood up and held his throat.

I happened to be in the same restaurant. I went over to the stigmatic and enabler caller.

In front of our tables of similarity I said, "So, you enabler caller, you have a hard piece of food in your throat."

"It's a big piece of steak. Help him, help him. We don't know what to do," said Mrs. Mantes.

"Do you need my help, Mr. Mantes? Can you get the piece of steak blocking your breathing out yourself? Come on, you can breathe, try harder to breathe with that lodged piece of meat causing all your awful symptoms. Pull yourself up and just do it yourself. Are you scared, anxious, panicking, and unable to do anything? Yes, I'm sure you are," I said.

"Do something, Mrs. Patstegre. If you don't help him, he might die," Mrs. Mantes screamed.

"You feel out of control, Mr. Mantes. This fear and out of control feeling you are experiencing is because *You can't do it*, right? This is what people suffering from mental illness feel. They *can't* do things because of their illness.

"I will now do the Heimlich maneuver to help you because you need help and *can't do it by yourself*. Oh wait, maybe you should try a little harder to breathe on your own and get the piece of steak out of your throat. Are you paralyzed with fear that there is no one that will help you? Will you call me an enabler if I help you? Maybe I should wait until you feel like if I don't help you that you might die. No. I will help you," I said.

As Mr. Mantes started to breathe, he looked in my eyes. I stared back at the stigma spreader.

"I am not an enabler. I am a helper," I said.

"I'm sorry Mrs. Patstegre. You are correct. I felt out of control, anxious beyond anything I have ever felt, and feared for my life, something I also haven't felt before. If I had to feel strong fear, panic, and fierce stress like that every day, it would be hard to function.

"I now have a better understanding of what people that suffer from mental illness go through. I am forever changed. I will never call a Caregiver, an enabler. Again, I am very sorry for the pain I caused you," Mr. Mantes said.

That was the end of my teaching story. I used the example of choking to illustrate the difference between, *I can't do something* and *I won't do something.*

I put my pen down. Yes, I wrote the old-fashioned way today.

I tried to relax the rest of the day.

I decided to prepare food for Hookum, the soup kitchen. I would be volunteering in a couple of days.

Diary Entry 45 - November 30

"Hi Gus," I said.

"Hi Mrs. Patstegre," he said.

Gus stared at me. Did he think I was calm? Was he thinking I might be young because I had few wrinkles, a couple of streaks of gray hair, and no sunspots. I was not a sunworshipper.

I stared back at Gus. Many times, I felt Mr. Patstegre's spirit walking with me and protecting me. This was one of those times.

Gus was a smart, something not right, college boy that had intellect and wit.

Why did Gus give up his time to volunteer? Was he a product of Mommy and Daddy problems? Did he blame everything on his parents like some millennials did?

Gus was cutting bread with his back to me. I had just taken out one of the casseroles from the oven. As I walked toward the chipped and faded white counter, I banana slipped in Gus's direction. My Pyrex rectangle of pasta slid into Gus's forearm. There must have been some water on the floor.

"Shit, what are you doing Mrs. Patstegre?" exclaimed brown balding twenty something to be determined, Gus.

I saw a very reactive Gus. He was an alphabet screamer going from A to Z with all telling speed.

"I am so sorry, Gus. I didn't mean it. It was an accident. The pan barely touched you," I said.

I put the casserole down on the counter. I looked at his arm.

"Once again, I'm sorry, Gus. Fortunately, it just nipped you. It's not even red. Run your arm under cold water. That will help. You can also hold ice on it just to play it safe. I don't think it is necessary," I said.

Gus appeared to be a cry baby. Not the cool, tough guy he acted like.

Gus had peeped his Tom personality to me. He was a hot head. He was secretive.

I was an air of agony, someone who barely breathed, and had pain as her pronoun.

I took a couple of deep breaths.

Gus was quiet for the rest of the day.

We fed everyone, cleaned up in silence, and left at separate times.

Diary Entry 46 - December 2

More and more people were riding under my fingernails. I was getting edgy.

I did something against my grain. I started to look at myself. I saw the lost person I was. I wanted at least part of me back.

Caregivers like me could not keep walking a high wire, all the time without thinking of their needs. We got tired and run down. When we got in this beat up, bruised, holey clothes, and lack of care for ourselves state, we lost the name on our birth certificates.

I needed help. I wanted help. I needed to rid myself of my *spin the world* stress and anguish. I needed to live with a little sadness, enough to shed some tears.

I dropped into bed with my baggy night shirt on and snuggled under by red down quilt.

"Talking Ceiling are you there?" I asked.

"Yes, Mrs. Patstegre," Talking Ceiling answered.

"I have a desire to feel better, look better, and be better. If I get help from someone, will they go too fast to try to faucet out my feelings? Will my heart speed up? Will my blood pressure elevate? I might not be ready to handle the sorrow and loss," I said.

"Mrs. Patstegre, I won't let you proceed into anything that I don't think you can handle. I will help you in any way I can. I want the best for you," Talking Ceiling said.

"Thank you, Talking Ceiling. That is comforting. I'm grateful for your good heartedness. I'm touched by your tenderness. And I'm excited by your eagerness to help," I said.

Talking Ceiling didn't say anything else. I yawned and I drifted to sleep.

Diary Entry 47 - December 4

I swallowed the notion of exploring my emotions.

I made an appointment with a psychotherapist, another name for a talk therapist, thereby increasing my job responsibilities to include being a Client of Ms. Lee.

I sat in the waiting room at Ms. Lee's office. She sensed urgency in my voice when I called to make an appointment. She got me in soon after I called her.

I pretended to read a magazine with the other people waiting to be summoned up the stairs.

"Mrs. Patstegre, Ms. Lee is ready for you. She is located at the top floor of the L-shaped stairs, first door on the left," the receptionist said.

I walked up the green and blue checked carpet lined stairs. There were red speckles in the carpet. I stopped my mind from imagining what the red speckles might be.

I knocked on the white semi-gloss painted door. The door had an old-fashioned key lock below the doorknob.

"Come in," said a faceless Ms. Lee.

I opened the door. There sat an elderly woman with ageless skin and polar bear hair. She wore green framed glasses. I saw an old blue jean jacket on a chair next to her desk. I liked that.

We sat down on two brown leather chairs. The matching chairs were across from each other. I wondered how many had sat there previously. I tried to tell myself that Ms. Lee was here to help me. Could I really share anything of substance with her? Didn't I have to get to know this woman a little before the revealing process started?

I thought the conversation with Ms. Lee might be salt, pepper, thyme, and other spices. We would mouth back and forth about small things. It seemed like the meat, main course, lasagna of my life would stay in Neverland.

"I am Ms. Lee. I am glad you decided to come here for help," Ms. Lee said.

I wore running shoes and exercise clothes to this appointment, making it easier to leave and run to Bessie.

"Is there something you want to talk about?" Ms. Lee asked.

"Yes. Yesterday I went to…and did…and was with…," I answered.

As I talked, I knew I was doing myself a disservice. The question became, would I keep this facade up or would I let this lovely woman eventually help me? After all, if she was good, which I believed she was, she already knew a little about me from my superficial, waste of time conversation that I just told her.

I left. Cold. I was always cold. I took a hot shower when I got home.

Diary Entry 48 - December 5

Christmas was coming close to claiming its day. Christmas was a glorious time for many, a miserable time for some.

I decided to go outside. There was a dark peace around me. I started out walking. I lifted to a special sleigh ride. Destination was care.

Call this a fairy tale. Call it a flight of hope. Call it an imaginary insight.

"Dispatching, calling all Caregivers, calling all Sufferers, I, Mrs. Patstegre will deliver some act of compassion tonight. I will cheerlead and pom-pom until the day I die for people suffering from mental illness. May I live into my hundreds. After that, in Caregiving Heaven, I will continue paying attention to loved ones that suffer from mental and physical illness on earth," I said.

My flight of hope landed. I was sitting next to someone suffering from anxiety, depression, mania, and psychosis in an emergency room. His name was Oscar. He was waiting for well-intended and smart psychiatrists to make the best diagnosis for many scary symptoms. Criss cross applesauce symptoms were abundant for Oscar from triggers known and unknown.

"Oscar, I'm Mrs. Patstegre, would you like to talk?"

A sleepy, sedated Oscar blinked which I took as a yes.

"Oscar, I am not a delusion. I am a Caregiver. I want you to know that someone cares about what you are going through. I am a constant novena in your life. You are not alone.

"Reach out and you will feel a breeze of relief, a gust of hope, and a storm of strength. May these winds be your stent to free-flowing knowledge of your illness and willingness to find a doctor, practice coping skills, and work with a loved one who will help you," I said.

"I want to believe you. I really do," Oscar said.

"You can believe me. If you have doubts, try thinking in a stimulus response way. When you feel wind blowing at your face and body, know that a Caregiver is thinking of you and sending you a gust of hope and a storm of strength. You will know that you are not alone," I said.

"My Dad died a couple of years ago. Every time I see a squirrel in my back yard, I know it is my dad. He lets me know that he is still here with me. Sometimes that squirrel will look at me, stay still when I approach it, and not fear my presence. He even eats my plants, and I let him. I don't shoo him away like I have done with chipmunks and squirrels in the past.

"My Dad always liked my cooking when he visited, so the squirrel eating my plants is rewarding to me. I know my

Dad is telling me that he misses me. Is that what you are talking about?" Oscar asked.

"Yes, it is Oscar," I answered.

Oscar smiled. He slumbered. Visiting hours had been over for a couple of hours in the emergency room.

"Good-bye, Oscar. I must tiptoe out of your room. Remember you are not alone," I said.

I smuggled myself out. I vanished. I sleighed. I smiled.

It was a good night.

Diary Entry 49 - December 7

My sister, Effie, lived alone. She was on her way over to stay for a week during the Holidays.

I reminded Effie of her inner desire to do things well. With a little prodding, Effie fought like the dickens to get the job done.

Two incidents showing one of Effie's greatest strengths, doing things well, was boldly seen in the following stories. Both stories were different in texture and appearance, but the final arrangement ended the same.

Effie - Story One

It was a summer day when this story began. The sun warmed a tree lined bike path with shades of purple shadows. The path of peaceful high was twelve feet wide and twenty-five miles long.

"We have arrived. Let's rollerblade with strides of heads up and feet down. I will accept a few feet up, bottom down, and roll around falls. I promised you I would shoehorn your roller blades on, lace them up, and tie double knotted bows," I said.

"Mrs. Patstegre, I don't know why you do this to me. You don't listen. You just want someone to go with you, talk and talk and talk, and do exactly what you want them to do. I'm staying in the car. You go," Effie said.

I waited for the reactive words to keep going, instead she stayed quiet.

I took a pair of rollerblades that Speet wore when he was young that looked like they would fit her. They were in good condition.

I decided to bribe Effie so she could experience the freedom of gliding.

"Effie, we can stop and get a milk shake at a deli right off the bike path, a couple miles away. Also, I promise not to talk or get you to engage. I will let you concentrate on rollerblading," I said.

"Alright, you won't take no for an answer so I will try. Do I have to wear all that stuff you have on the floor of Bessie?" Effie asked.

"You do have to put on the elbow pads, the knee pads, and the helmet which comprises the things you call stuff. I will wear all the same protection. Rollerblading a few times makes me an understudy, not a star," I answered.

I helped Effie dress for her bike path appearance. She looked stage ready. I did the same. I helped her out of the front seat.

"Effie, with your five-foot height and blue eyes, can you please put your right rollerblade on the foot holder of Bessie. Come on, hold on to my shoulders. Now, let your right rollerblade drop down to the ground, and then lean on me, to get your other rollerblade to the ground," I said.

Success! We both stood on the ground. We walked sideways down the little hill to the bike trail. I held on to her.

We were on the bike trail. We were holding each other. Road runners and bicyclists ran and cycled past with an on the left signal. I wondered if they thought we were in love, holding each other, or just a couple of old people trying to act young.

"Jerks, they shouldn't go that fast," Effie said.

We looked down the path and then looked at each other.

"Let's begin," I said.

Fast forward a couple of months. We rollerbladed at least once a week since our first run. We were on the bike trail again on another sunny day. The following was what her spirit revealed to me.

"Mrs. Patstegre, we have glided ten miles. Can we rollerblade another ten?" Effie asked.

"You realize if we do that, we will have to rollerblade twenty miles back to Bessie," I answered.

Her shoulders moved like a little kid excited to go ten extra miles. She jumped up and down, rollerblades and all. I knew that she was serious. Confident that she could do it, who was I to take that youthful energy from her.

Before I could say anything, Effie saved me.

"You have a good point. It is ten miles back to Bessie at this point. If we go another ten, we will both be too tired to race back to Bessie. Let's go, Mrs. Patstegre. I will race you," Effie said.

"Okay," I said.

This wonderful outlaying of pure feeling good about oneself was picturesque. The how to achieve feeling good might have been a thesis topic to do in my psychology years in college. Grant money would have been spent well to learn the formula of this feel-good mixture.

What made Effie metamorphous into strong and determined Effie? Why such opposition to start something?

Was it fear of failure? Maybe.

What I knew and saw was when Effie got up and got going, she became good, and then great at what she did. She became the Queen of Rollerblading.

Effie - Story Two

How much wood could an Effie chuck, chuck?

The ranchers on *Gunsmoke, Bonanza, and Yellowstone* had not seen a ranch hand handle wood like Effie.

It was cold outside. The whole afternoon Effie and I wanted to make a fire in the fireplace in the TV room.

"Come on. Let's get the wood to build that fire that we both want," Effie said.

I was speechless and taken by surprise. Effie was the motivator. I, by default, became the follower. I followed her stride with pleasure and delight.

I pulled my rusty wheelbarrow off the back of the house, where it was leaning. It was fifty years old. It worked great. Effie took the wagon next to the wheelbarrow.

Effie pulled an old-fashioned, red wagon behind her. She was walking at a fast metronome speed toward the wood pile located in the backyard.

"Hey, Effie, wait for me," I said.

She did not. I sped up, twisting my ankle a little on a mole hole. I got to the wood pile with my wheelbarrow. Effie started putting the cut logs in her wagon as fast as she could.

"Effie, slow down. Your golden, strong arms are throwing the logs into the wagon faster than I knew possible," I said.

"Hurry up, Mrs. Patstegre," Effie said.

"I am. I can't throw them as far and as fast as you. I will pile them up in my wheelbarrow as fast as I can," I said.

Effie had ten to fifteen logs of wood in her wagon. She started up a slight incline in the lawn pulling her wagon behind her. She stopped at the bottom of a couple of cement steps, leading to the log hoop on the back porch.

I parked my wheelbarrow full of logs next to her wagon. We started carrying the logs up the stairs. We put them in the log hoop made of solid iron. Was Effie going to take two steps at a time? No, she played it safe. She blended it up at a fast speed, though.

This was good old fashioned hard work done by Effie. This goodness/greatness wanted to come out. Effie usually shunned from attention. This time she wanted to be seen and applauded. A wonderful show to watch. A five-star rating.

How many people waiting, already had a number, and wanted their number to be called? Endless amounts of people wanted and needed to be noticed. Paying attention to someone was catching. Once you saw the magic behind the attention paid, you became a habitual attention giver.

Diary Entry 50 - December 9

Caregiving, Cooking, Cleaning, being a Client, and Mind Killing were necessary unions of survival jobs for me.

Cunning cleverness enhanced my creativity in everything I did.

Covers that matched their books were rare but sought after. They deserved to stand out.

Diary Entry 51 - December 10

I decided last night I would make a trip to Concerned Care Nursing Home today. I didn't want to wait until January. All my Lovelies were lonely during the Holidays.

It was icy outside. Bessie and I slid part of the way to the Nursing Home.

I ran past the front desk. Crystal was not there, probably helping someone. I'll see her on the way out.

My twenty wonderful aging people that I saw here were precious. I treasured them.

I loaded my Care-Cart with medically approved snacks, magazines, newspapers, all the usual things. Today I added small Christmas trees. They were twelve inches high, five inches wide, with a two-inch diameter wood base. The green pine trees had splashes of silver attached to their needles.

I was surprised how much I missed talking with my Lovelies. Ms. File and Mr. Gaudan were my favorites, even though I loved and cared for all of them.

"Good morning, good morning, good morning to all," I said.

Everyone took something from my gray cart. Most kept the holiday tree next to them on their nightstand or dresser.

I wheeled my cart down the corridor. Once again, out of the corner of my eye, I saw a familiar looking person, flash past me, and push open the door to the stairs. Who was that?

The flash came to me. It looked like Gus, my volunteer partner, at the Hookum Soup Kitchen.

I was outside Ms. File's room. I knocked.

"Come in," Ms. File said.

"It's you, Mrs. Patstegre. I'm so excited to see you," Ms. File said.

"I'm glad to see you, too, Ms. File. I see that you painted two more paintings. Is this painting of a dog for someone that you know?" I asked.

"Yes, it is. It is for one of my favorite students who comes by to see me routinely. I am so grateful for his friendship. I painted this for him. I hope he likes it," Ms. File answered.

"Oh, Ms. File, the colors are wonderful, it's painted well, and the dog's face is priceless," I said.

"Thank you, Mrs. Patstegre, for your complements," Ms. File said.

"What can I get you from the Care-Cart today?" I asked.

"I will take a *Wall Street Journal, The New York Times,* and *Forbes,*" Ms. File answered.

"Here you are Ms. File. I brought these small Christmas trees. I know the trees aren't real, but I wanted all of you to have a little Holiday cheer. You can put it anywhere in your room," I said.

"I am lucky, Mrs. Patstegre, to have someone like you. The Christmas trees will make many here happy, especially those that get few visitors. My former students have become my family, come often, and especially remember me around Christmas," Ms. File said.

"Speaking of family, wintertime reminds me of Mr. Patstegre. I wish he was still with us. I busy it up to stop thinking processes that may not be beneficial for me. Mr. Patstegre and I were two lenses, connected by a sturdy frame. We saw things with clarity and speed. I miss that," I said.

"Mrs. Patstegre, you are kind and it's sad that Mr. Patstegre departed too soon. I can listen and help you if you would let me," Ms. File said.

"Thank you, Ms. File. Maybe you can help someone else. Ms. File, you know Mr. Gaudan, right?" I asked.

"Yes, he is down the hall from me. He is quiet and keeps to himself. I don't know much else about him," Ms. File answered.

"I know his family does not visit often. Would you mind walking with me down the hall to say hello to him?" I asked.

"Sure. I can take a little walk to introduce myself to Mr. Gaudan. Let's go," Ms. File answered.

Ms. File got up. She was dressed in black. I loved that about her. She had matching black clogs, which told me she was a hot shit. Her hair was white and straight with a ruby hair pin on one side. I thought she was beautiful. She was a role model to admire and follow.

"Oh, by the way, I think I saw someone leave your room today," I said.

"You did, Mrs. Patstegre. His name is Gus. I taught him in high school. Shortly after Gus graduated, I retired from teaching. Gus is a smart young man. As a matter of fact, he went on to study the law or law enforcement. I want to say that he works as a private investigator but I am not sure. I can ask him next time if you want me to," Ms. File said.

"That would be great, Ms. File. Thank you," I said.

Gus lied. I knew it. His true occupation explained his inquisitive nature. I was fearful that his intuitive skills could somehow see my vivid, real-like mind kills. Of course, that was impossible.

We walked down the cheerful hallway to Mr. Gaudan's room. We knocked. He told us to come in.

"Good morning, Mr. Gaudan. I brought newspapers and whatever else you might want. I was wondering if Ms. File could come in with me. She wanted to get out of her room and walk with me. I told her I had one more stop. I brought you a small Christmas tree for a little cheer," I said.

"I'm not suitable for a visitor. Look at Ms. File. She is so well dressed. I'm disheveled," Mr. Gaudan said.

"Mr. Gaudan, thank you for your compliment. I am down the hall from you. I taught history, never got married, and any visitors you see are former students. They are my family, my only family. May I sit down?" Ms. File asked.

Mr. Gaudan was silent, so we took that as a yes. I helped Ms. File into a chair near Mr. Gaudan's look alike *Frasier's* Dad's recliner. They started talking.

I put Mr. Gaudan's pine tree and a *Wall Street Journal* on his table. I backed out in silence. I hoped that he would read his newspaper later.

I parked my Care-Cart in a corner in the supply room. I patted my cart goodbye and sailed past the front desk. Crystal was still not there. Maybe she had finals. I left a pine tree and a note for her on her desk. I left Concerned Care. A heavy snow greeted me.

Bessie and I enjoyed the ride home. I opened the window and felt the cold beauty on my face.

I turned on the news when I got home, then turned it off. Outer space had entered our newsrooms. I wanted to stay on Earth.

I called Clippy.

"What's up, Dawg!" Clippy said.

We both laughed every time she answered the phone like that.

"How is your back, Clippy?"

"My back is doing okay. I am forcing myself to sit and read to let my back get a break from walking. Women's bodies go through so much more than men's bodies. Men don't birth other human beings, so trauma is limited to our bodies. I had back labor delivering my children. That is why my back hurts so much," Clippy said.

"I'm glad you are taking care of your back. I agree with you that giving birth is tough on our bodies and especially for you. Then after all our childbearing years, menopause falls upon us. We ride the carousal of zebras with folds instead of stripes and tigers that wish they could scratch themselves instead of scarring others. And why is it called menopause instead of womenopause? Because men are supposed to take a pause and be nice to us? Maybe," I said.

"Mrs. Patstegre, I agree. I remember when I was young, I was pretty good looking. Maybe the pounds we put on as we age bother us because we know what it felt like to be thin and attractive when we were young," Clippy said.

"Clippy, I miss Mr. Patstegre. He didn't care about those superficial things. He looked at me in that special way. He opened the car door for me and gently put his hand on my lower back and pushed me in front of him when we walked into our favorite restaurant. He knew I appreciated the gentleman in him. Many times, he kissed me like it was the first day that we met. He saw me as an aging beauty," I said.

"See Mrs. Patstegre, you were a lucky Daaaawg to have such a nice and loving husband. I wasn't lucky. Mine strayed. I tell you all the time that I don't want another man. I don't want to go through all that shit again. Maybe that's why I swear so much. Oh, who cares. I am who I am and that's that. Besides, my Mom needs care every day so I don't have time for a man. Hell, I barely get to see you and you are my best friend," Clippy said.

"When your ex gets older, he will realize what he gave up. He is an idiot. Thirty years of marriage and he decides to run after young trash," I said.

"I swear and yell at people who bug me. I tell it like it is. I talk to people, but they exhaust me. Besides you and a few others, I have little patience for anyone. I am a true introvert. I tell people to shut the hell up. I don't give a shit what they think. I know you carry resentment like me. Try and swear more," Clippy said.

"Clippy, I swear some days. I act silly and do other things to help myself. I believe angels hold my hands. Angels push me up from the used to be springboard floors. They shine lights for me to drive Bessie better at night. Bessie's lights are not as bright as the LED ones on the newer cars. I think Mr. Patstegre is an angel that stands by me and helps me many days," I said.

"Mrs. Patstegre, you are my dear friend and I love you. You think way too much about everything. Who cares the reason for anything, I say. I know you want to get into your favorite blue jeans again. I do too.

"The difference between you and me is I really don't care about how I look. Maybe I do a little. It is what it is and to hell with anyone that argues with me. I eat what I want, and I'll yell at someone who tells me not to. I am sticking up for myself. I am taking care of me," Clippy said.

"Clippy, you're right. I need to take better care of myself. Eventually, women rock climb over everything to help themselves. I'm working on starting that move. I want to find those stable rocks up the mountains of magnitude and start climbing," I said.

"Mrs. Patstegre, rest that thinking mind of yours before I come over and yell at you," Clippy said.

"I will Clippy. Goodbye. Love you."

"Love you more, Mrs. Patstegre."

Diary Entry 52 - December 12

Sometimes nothing worked to de-escalate a situation. I
tried and tweaked. I jumped and jolted. I pencil-sharpened
my listening skills. Then, I discovered something that
worked most of the time. I called it Tone Sharpening.

Tone Sharpening was answering a question, responding
with my own words in the same tone that the person/loved
one used with me. The hope was that the person who
started the conversation with a hostile tone would hear the
same hostile tone from me and pause in their response.

An example of Tone Sharpening went something like the
following:

Someone suffering from irritability and restlessness asked,
"WHAT do you MEEEEEEAAAAAN, Mrs. Patstegre?"

"I Meeeeeeaaaaan, that WE need to LEAVE soon to get to
your appointment," I answered.

I was employed in the developmental department of life.
Tone Sharpening was one of those developments. Being
open minded to invent different things to desensitize a
situation was important. This helped me see what things
worked and what didn't.

This awareness moved me to clear counters of clutter. I
kept patterns, words, tones, and actions that worked in
different knowledge squares of my imaginary, Caregiving
quilt. This quilt, held together with love, was an advocate

of experience and a never-ending capital campaign to care for and find a cure for all suffering from mental illness.

Diary Entry 53 - December 13

I decided late this afternoon to go to my cousin, Daisy's house.

Daisy worked in an office full time. I didn't see her very often. Daisy's talents existed in the right and left sides of her brain.

Being a finance manager Daisy made numbers work in many ways. She dressed those numbers up with her flare for fashion. Her blond hair with green streaks did not cover a ditzy person's head. It covered a smart, got things done person's brain. She spit fire like no other dragon, moved fast, and finished storms of projects when we worked together.

I knocked on the door. No answer.

"Daisy, are you in there?" I yelled.

I held my mouth along the crack of the door and yelled again to see if she was home.

Kai pushed his face against a window in the living room and looked at me.

"Is your Mom home?" I asked.

He nodded his head. I took that to mean yes.

"Let me in please," I said.

The doorknob turned and Kia let me in. I patted his dark, thick layered hair. Daisy had adopted Kia as a single Mother. She had decided that marriage was not in the cards for her. She was a good Mother.

"She is upstairs. Go on up," Kai said.

I ran up the stairs and found Daisy organizing her closet. She had many lists. She had a knack for organization.

"Daisy, I was wondering if you want to go out tonight," I said.

"I'm in the middle of a project. Unless it is an emergency, I would like to finish," Daisy said.

"You are surrounded by clothes of different sizes, all sorts of funky shoes, and purses, all screaming to move them to a more comfortable place on the shelf. They need to be seen and used. They feel neglected. You need to do this project today," I said.

I hugged Daisy, waved good-bye to Kai, and sat in good old Bessie.

"Well, Bessie, we have a good forty-five minutes until we get home. Daisy is too busy to come out with us," I said.

Daisy hadn't walked in my shoes. My shoes walked in a one plus one equals three line. Her shoes walked in a one plus one equals two line. Her black and whiteness view of the world conflicted with my very colorful life.

Tonight, I wanted and needed to zig zag my mind and heart pain into a straight line of thinking to accomplish goodness.

Why did some people in this world suffer from pain more than others? Life was unfair said the majority. Life was unfair and I wanted to do something about it said me.

December was a month of giving. There was a warehouse named CQHS, three or four miles up the road. They made warm coats, quilts, hats, and scarfs. I wanted warmth for the homeless.

Hopefully, I could convince the manager of CQHS to give me some of their coats and other products for the homeless that were seconds.

Mr. Patstegre worked for CQHS before he died. He knew the CEO, Mr. Antas. That might help me sway the night manager to part with some seconds that were scheduled to go to the discount stores. I knew they worked round the clock.

"Okay, Bessie, we are going to stop at a factory up the street. I want to distribute their warm products to the homeless. I hope they will help us," I said.

I said a prayer that the manager would be kind and generous tonight.

We slowed down. We parked. Bessie turned her lights off.

"Now behave yourself, Bessie. I sense a little mischief brewing from you," I said.

In front of me was an old warehouse with aches and pains on its walls. I opened a heavy, steal-dented door. I walked in. The door slammed behind me.

"Good evening, everyone. My name is Mrs. Patstegre. I advocate for the forgotten homeless. They suffer every day. They are forced into bad luck beds of coldness. They have weathered skin, tattered clothes, and little or no care," I said.

A tall young man with kind eyes approached me.

"I am the night manager, Mr. Antas. I overheard your speech," he said.

"My husband, Mr. Patstegre, did work for a Mr. Antas who was the CEO, a while ago. You look too young to be him. Are you related?" I asked.

"Yes, I am. I am Abe Antas. I believe the man you are referring to is my Uncle Bernard Antas. He is still the CEO of this company," Abe Antas answered.

"Thanks for the clarification. It is nice to meet you," I said.

"It is nice to meet you, too. I volunteer to work extra hours the four weeks before the Holidays to give managers time off to be with their families. I am also the one in charge of dropping off seconds to charities in need of our products," Abe said.

"May I take some of your irregular items of clothing and distribute them to the homeless? Your coats and blankets will save lives this time of the year. I volunteer at the Hookum Soup Kitchen and serve many of the homeless meals. I would love to give them your products to make the cold more bearable for them," I said.

"It would be my pleasure to help you and the homeless," Abe said.

"Thank you for your generosity. I am grateful," I said.

Abe had a stare that shivered me into thinking that he carried secrets. I guessed he might have a loved one lost on the streets.

Abe helped me load Bessie with quilts, coats, scarfs, mittens, and hats. I shook his hand and thanked him again.

I waved good-bye.

I handed out comfort tonight to the homeless. The eyes of unison, all seeing the value of the deed, sent silent looks of thanks to me. I felt warm inside.

I would let Abe know how much his generosity meant to so many.

"Bessie let's go home. Daisy, my cousin, missed a good night full of happiness."

Diary Entry 54 - December 14

Speet wanted to go off to school, play music, or do both. He needed to know how I felt about him leaving. I was worried. Was he ready to be on his own? Could he handle anxiety felt from his trauma away from the safety of his home?

Primer paint and long underwear were synonymous with Caregiving. Those under garments or first layers, like Caregiving, helped prepare young adults for life outside the safety that they desired and were used to.

Caregivers were the pre-trial, getting those that suffer from mental illness ready for the outside world. We gave them important information for the deposition of life. They would face prosecutions, persecuting mouths screaming words of stigma and hurt, and grueling juries and judges.

Imagine the courage and coping skills loved ones suffering from mental illness and Caregivers needed to defend themselves every day!

Not everyone showed discrimination; I found the majority did when it came to mental illness.

I tried to prepare loved ones suffering from mental illness to spot hand movements, eye flitters, phrases missed by others, and odd subtle things that said watch out, it was a lie, they were not who they said they were. I tried to teach loved ones to read the sign language of the situation, not just see what was happening around them.

Caregiving, teaching, and respective relationships formed unbreakable bonds.

As advocates, protectors, and fighters, Caregivers wouldn't ever be held in contempt of court. Our love was never under the gavel of others. Never.

Diary Entry 55 - December 15

I wasn't an Our Father, who Art in Heaven kind of writer. I didn't have an English degree. I majored in Psychology centering my classes around an A game. Why shouldn't I have an A degree in anger? It wasn't my nature to settle for a B.

The other night, distributing warmth to the homeless produced niceness. Tonight, highlights of dark on dark were felt throughout my body. Words like shit, damn, and asshole were high on my vocabulary list.

Dark on dark existed in me because I wanted my A plus anger to be noticed. Notice relaxed the constant gag reflex I lived with. My anger had to come out and it did through mind killing. Horror hovered in my mind killing dreams. Terror pierced my grieving heart and allowed that hole to release feelings.

I found myself wanting to talk with Talking Ceiling. I went upstairs and laid on my bed. Talking Ceiling was wide eyed.

"Talking Ceiling, sometimes Christmas time is rough on my sister, Effie. She is spending time at my house. She doesn't want to be alone. I sense Effie's anger, after all I sense mine all the time," I said.

"Mrs. Patstegre, are you worried that you might mind kill tonight? Do you want to work out some of Effie's issues along with yours?" Talking Ceiling asked.

"I'm not sure, maybe," I answered.

"Talking Ceiling, six months ago, Effie broke up with her boyfriend, Martin. He was abusive to her for years. He drank. Effie tried to help him.

"Effie begged Martin to go to a psychiatrist. She offered to pay for his appointments and go with him. His addiction overpowered listening. Nothing worked. Martin got worse, drinking every night. That was when his pain got abusive with rageful words and actions. She finally left him," I said.

"It seems like Effie suffered as well as her ex-boyfriend, Martin. Are you afraid of where your dreams will lead you tonight?" Talking Ceiling asked.

"Yes," I answered.

"Well, close your eyes. You might surprise yourself. You say your mind kills might not be occurring as much. However, I think you might slip back to your mind killing dreams when things become overwhelming again. I could be wrong. Now please drift into sleep and let's see what happens," Talking Ceiling said.

"Okay, Talking Ceiling," I said.

Like with my other mind kills, I fell into a deep sleep.

I found myself reaching out to Effie in my dream.

"Effie, do you want to release your hurt? If yes, let's go on your first hurting hunt.

"Christmas trees are in my heart and tinsel tinseling in my toes and fingers. Ornamentally, the lights will brighten the path you want to take. Are holidays of grief going to follow you like a private detective?" I asked.

"Am I going to listen to your interruption of the English language tonight? Are you going to say how you wish you had gotten a Ph.D. if I go with you? And even though you can talk about anything, you talk about finding justice for and decreasing the stigma associated with mental illness.

"Do you do that because you don't think I can handle the unhappiness that you carry? See, I can tell by the way you looked at me that my comment was right. Am I going to be exhausted as an introvert just being with you?" Effie answered in a questioning way.

"I thought about telling her no and calling her a short-tempered, trigger-happy hoarder, but I didn't. Instead, I said, "No Effie. You can be the boss. I will be the employee. I will be under your command while we ride in Bessie tonight. Is it a deal?" I asked.

"Deal," Effie answered.

"You're the boss, Effie. It's your decision what direction we go. I will put the tinsel, lights, and anything I think we might need in Bessie," I said.

"Okay," Effie said.

Effie directed me where to drive. We arrived at Martin's small, run down house. Effie picked this house because she was in command. Martin, her ex, stole her self-esteem, especially toward the end of their relationship when his alcohol addiction became abusive.

We approached Martin's back door. Effie knew the floor plan.

We wore black wool, pull over masks exposing our eyes, nose, and mouth. I think we last used these masks to shovel snow when it was ten degrees.

Effie and I carried our supplies in backpacks.

"Mrs. Patstegre, follow me. We will go through the kitchen door. There is an A shaped piece of window missing in the door. I can reach my hand through the opening, turn the lock, and let us in," Effie said.

Martin was in bed. He looked dead. He was on his back. Each one of his arms hung on either side of his sheetless, twin bed. The bed pad on the mattress was filthy. His almost six-foot frame was clothed with blue jeans and what at one time was a white t-shirt.

"He is passed out drunk," Effie said.

Within minutes, Effie and I emptied our backpacks on the floor. We wrapped Martin's body, minus his head, with sticky cellophane. He laid without making a sound.

"Should we make Martin look like a Christmas tree?" I asked.

"Yes, tree decorating will be illuminating!!!! Ha, Ha. I sound like you, Mrs. Patstegre. Maybe secretly, I would like to be like you. No, you like to communicate too much. Do you talk to yourself? You are probably one of those that talk to yourself in the grocery store, saying that you need this and that for your recipe," Effie said.

"You can be mean mouthed, Effie. Let's keep going," I said.

We wrapped a strand of a hundred lights around his cellophaned body. All different colors …. a *Sargent Pepper's* trip of happiness for Effie. Martin never moved an inch.

"Effie, do you want to tinsel wrap him, too?" I asked.

"Sure," Effie answered.

We draped the thick, gold tinsel the best we could over his cellophaned body.

Anger anguished inside of Effie and me. It subwayed up and down our bodies.

I tried to drift my mind away from disgusting thoughts of protection for Effie, like we should staple gun the tinsel to Martin and hook ornaments through his fingernails, more holes a plenty and tears of blood. After all, those thoughts brought dignity to my anger.

My mind continued to wander. I took a deep breath and reeled in any other ideas of puncturing pain.

Imagination allowed my feelings to be heard. Fury fueled my fight for change and at the same time indirectly comforted the misery Effie went through.

I felt Effie needed me to help her deal with her emotions concerning Martin.

Suddenly, Effie stepped back and said, "Martin looks old. Physically, he is still a young man. The two deep sad lines around his mouth show me that he needs help. I don't want to hurt him; I want to help him."

I looked at Martin to see if I saw what she saw. Visions of days and nights filled with black out drinking and dread dashed in front of my eyes. There were many wrinkles of addiction on his face.

I felt sorry for him, too. Addiction needed support. I knew that inside. My need to protect Effie clouded my caring thoughts of helping Martin. Mind killing was unnecessary.

"Will you help me unwrap Martin, Mrs. Patstegre?" Effie asked.

"Yes, I will," I answered.

We removed everything from Martin's body. He barely moved. Maybe he was paralyzed from loss of hope. Maybe the numbing alcohol allowed him to sleep.

Effie and I left through the same door that we entered.

"I will call Martin next week. I will talk to him and let him know that I was thinking of him. I will forgive him for his past behavior toward me," Effie said.

"I'm tired. Can you take me home, Mrs. Patstegre?" Effie asked.

"Yes, Effie," I answered.

We headed toward Effie's apartment.

Everyone needed care. Effie forgave. Were somethings forgivable and somethings not forgivable? It was up to the individual and the situation was my answer.

"Would you like to stop at Jack's Diner and get a diet coke and a cheeseburger?" Effie asked.

I nodded yes. We stopped at the diner.

"I will have a cheeseburger, fries, and a diet coke. Do you want the same Mrs. Patstegre?" Effie asked.

"Sure," I answered.

Effie looked around.

"Mrs. Patstegre, I don't feel tired anymore. I could talk all night. Maybe I should order some coffee," Effie said.

"Mrs. Patstegre, you are in for a long night," I whispered to myself.

I woke up.

Talking Ceiling was sleeping. I would tell her later that a mind killing dream turned into heartfelt care.

Diary Entry 56 - December 18

Gifts for holidays and birthdays did not have to be bought. Sometimes, I used creative poems and writings for gifts.

What was the definition of a poem? Creative words of communication was a poem.

I found that anyone who received a poem or creative writing, bringing attention to their talents, appreciated it. I used the old-fashioned method of printing my poems out and framing the hard copies. E-mailing, texting, social media, whatever the newest fad of communication, could be used to relay your special gift to loved ones.

The following poem could be used as a stencil by applying your own words instead of the underlined words, thereby sparking creativity.

Smile when you think of your talents.

Smile when you think of your good habits.

Smile when you look inside your heart.

Smile at your integrity and competitive parts.

Smile with humor in every way.

Smile at yourself every day.

Act on your talents.

Act on your good habits.

Act when you look inside your heart.

Act with integrity and your competitive parts.

Act with humor in every way.

And Act on yourself every day.

Love, Mrs. Patstegre

The following acronym poem used Speet's name. I took each letter of his name and wrote about his uniqueness and his talents. Poems of kindness mattered. Paying attention to someone mattered.

Sport expertise
Priceless acts of kindness
Enormous talent on the guitar
Euphonic singing voice
Tons of writing ability

Diary Entry 57 - December 21

Cha Cha called me.

"Mrs. Patstegre, I'm afraid this time of year is depressing me. I appreciate your willingness to help me since my Mother died. Can I please see you, or can we talk on the phone?" Cha Cha asked.

"Of course, Cha Cha. Instead of talking on the phone now, how about coming with me to Ms. Lee, my therapist. I have an appointment today at three o'clock in the afternoon. This way we can all talk together," I answered.

Cha Cha hesitated.

"I don't want to intrude on your time with Ms. Lee," Cha Cha said.

"It's fine. I don't mind. I think Ms. Lee will be okay with it," I said.

"Well, okay," Cha Cha said.

"Good, I will pick you up at two o'clock this afternoon. We can talk on the way to my appointment," I said.

Cha Cha, Bessie, and I sat in Ms. Lee's parking lot. We were early. Cha Cha wore her depression hair style, the messy I don't care look which looked good on her. She fought spirals of depression and inner circles of anxiety. She was an attractive forty-year-old, even in this tough state of melancholy.

Could Ms. Lee remove nesting doll after nesting doll to get to the real me? Being a resistant client, I fought myself. I fought against everyone and everything. And now, I brought Cha Cha with me. Bringing Cha Cha was a way out for me and a way to help Cha Cha.

We entered Ms. Lee's office building.

The receptionist said for us to go up. We climbed the L-shaped staircase. Up six steps then a bigger seven. A right-angle to talk therapy.

"Good morning, Mrs. Patstegre. Who did you bring with you?" Ms. Lee asked.

"This is Cha Cha. I was friends with her Mother who passed away. She has no family. She needed help. I promised Cha Cha's Mother that I would help Cha Cha after she passed away. Ms. Lee, I was wondering if you could help her today. Helping Cha Cha will indirectly help me," I answered.

"I can talk with Cha Cha today. I do not want to make this a habit," Ms. Lee said.

"Thank you, Ms. Lee," I said.

My thoughts led me down the following path. If Ms. Lee said yes, she might be thinking that she could learn more about me from Cha Cha than from me. I admired that.

"Cha Cha, please start with what is on your mind," Ms. Lee said.

Cha Cha looked nervous.

Why did I go here? Maybe, I thought, if you combined a therapist with my experience, we could scrape brains of the best and tap the tree of syrupy feelings. Those could be challenging for someone like me, who preferred salt to sugar.

"Mrs. Patstegre helps me. I trust her. She pays attention to me and offers me tips. She accepts me without judgement," Cha Cha said.

"Mrs. Patstegre, can you tell us some of these tips?" Ms. Lee asked.

"Yes, I can. I try to get Cha Cha to become aware of her triggers that lead to unwanted symptoms such as restlessness and irritability. If a trigger such as not getting enough sleep is causing Cha Cha's symptoms of fear, poor insight, and stress, she needs to step back for a minute.

"She can take deep breathes, be aware of her surroundings, and accept her stress is high. If she doesn't fear from heightened sensitivity could produce panic," I answered.

"That is good insight, Mrs. Patstegre," Ms. Lee said.

"I miss my Mother. It is hard living alone. There are days that depression and anxiety take over. I am lucky to have someone like Mrs. Patstegre in my life. I appreciate her," Cha Cha said.

I squiggled in my usual chair. Ms. Lee had pulled up a third chair for Cha Cha that created a small circle of communication for today.

I couldn't talk about my feelings, only word them out. That was the challenge for me. Did Cha Cha agree to come to Ms. Lee to reveal things about me and not so much about her? Did Cha Cha stretch her melancholy because she noticed that I needed help from our phone calls?

Cha Cha continued her insights and comments.

"I want to reduce symptoms before they get too severe," Cha Cha said.

"That is a good thing, Cha Cha," Ms. Lee said.

"Ms. Lee, do I have time to explain a few triggers and symptoms that happen to me? Writing them down and saying them out loud, like Mrs. Patstegre taught me, makes me remember them more. I believe it will help me see how real my triggers and symptoms are," Cha Cha said.

"We have time. Please continue, Cha Cha," Ms. Lee said.

"Triggers are not just the result of my own behavior. Triggers can be caused by the behavior and experiences of others. Things just happen in life that are not my fault. The more I talk about my reactions the more I become familiar with them. I try to listen to others when they explain how they view my actions," Cha Cha said.

Cha Cha looked up.

"Please go on, Cha Cha," said Ms. Lee.

"Triggers for me can be doing too much or going to big events like a wedding, especially the out-of-town ones," Cha Cha said.

"Cha Cha, I find from speaking with clients that travel is a big trigger for them. I suggest to them if they must travel, especially to a destination wedding, not to attend pre-parties. I tell them to get as good a night sleep as possible by going to bed early.

"If you notice that you have too many symptoms like moodiness, heightened anxiety, poor insight, low energy or too much energy, you might want to consider not attending any big events that you have to travel for. As a matter of fact, sending a nicer wedding gift instead of attending a wedding or big event, might be a nice solution," Ms. Lee said.

"That sounds good, Ms. Lee. Thank you," Cha Cha said.

"Is there anything else that you would like to tell me?" Ms. Lee asked.

"Yes, there is. Mrs. Patstegre has a few mottos that she believes in. One of them is preparation is underrated. I try to be more prepared because of her," Cha Cha answered.

"I can see that Cha Cha. You seem prepared for this meeting today," Ms. Lee said.

"Mrs. Patstegre uses a business trio motto. Did I say that right Mrs. Patstegre?" Cha Cha asked.

"Yes," I answered.

"Cha Cha, I was wondering if Mrs. Patstegre can tell me about her business trio?" Ms. Lee asked.

"It's fine with me," Cha Cha answered.

"Go ahead, Mrs. Patstegre," Ms. Lee said.

"People close to a loved one can notice increasing symptoms from known triggers and unknown new triggers. I call attention to these symptoms that our loved one is experiencing. I call this first stage, *funny business*. This attention can help a loved one notice and diffuse their symptoms, such as irritability, restlessness, suspicion, sadness, and isolation.

"A loved one can use mindfulness, deep breaths, and coping mechanisms to de-escalate these funny business symptoms. If they don't de-escalate the funny business symptoms, then the second stage, *fearful business* symptoms can appear. If nothing is done to de-escalate the panic and fear, then the third stage, *delusional business* symptoms such as paranoia and psychosis can appear," I said.

"That is an intriguing business trio as you put it. I would like to discuss it more but we must stop here. Cha Cha, I can recommend someone for you to talk with if you are interested. You will be the only one coming to see me next time, right Mrs. Patstegre?" Ms. Lee asked.

"Yes, Ms. Lee. I will see you next time by myself," I answered.

I dropped Cha Cha off. She thanked me.

I parked Bessie in the garage. I went to my bedroom, threw my shoes off, and struck my usual back-pose on my bed.

"You know, Talking Ceiling, never let anyone sway you from helping and caring for the mentally ill and their needs. The mentally ill need us.

"Their distress causes symptoms of cognitive fog, impulsiveness, and tendencies to flee. These symptoms are not character traits of the one who suffers, they are symptoms. Why is that soooooooooo hard for people to understand?

"Hell Talking Ceiling, I go to meetings where people are irritable, unprepared and answer questions poorly. They are not mentally ill. What is their excuse? They want and choose to act that way. Someone who suffers from mental illness does not choose or want to exhibit the symptoms that mental illness spits out.

"Keep telling the truth, Talking Ceiling. Keep correcting the accusing enabling crowd, the know-it-all crowd, and the idiot crowd with stigmatic tongues of speech. Stop the tide of people that want to swallow hope," I said.

"Mrs. Patstegre, I hear you and I will do what you say. I will woo, protect, and glue eggshells back together for you," Talking Ceiling said.

"Talking Ceiling, it is up to us to care for our loved ones until their agendas, symptoms, and hard lives lead them in a coping way, a mindful way, and a survival way toward a better life.

"Cha Cha showed me today that what I do and what I help her with makes a difference.

"Caregivers know that getting help and maintaining help does not happen overnight with people who suffer from poor mental health. It can take years or decades. Fighting mental illness is an ongoing war, fought by the person suffering and their Caregivers," I said.

Diary Entry 58 - December 26

My mind wandered. It stopped on a familiar thought. Family, friends, outsiders, and the general population turned their mind and ears away from Caregivers' words and experiences. Seeing and believing things through their eyes was their belief system, rather than listening to valuable help from knowledgeable Caregivers. What a waste of time and energy.

On the contrary, I found that psychiatric nurses, friends who have a loved one with a mental illness, psychotherapists, psychologists, and psychiatrists all listened to and relied on the experience, opinions, and knowledge of Caregivers. That was where we received validity.

I roped in my high-spirited mind. I took that high spirit and tamed it on my piano. I ran my fingers up and down the eighty-eight black and white keys. A Bach C major composition or a Beethoven Sonatina were pieces in music books waiting for me to play them.

Playing the piano made my isolation come alive in a real way.

I curved my hands. I played, remembering what my music teacher, Sister Joseph Marie, instructed me to do. She told me never to let my wrists hang down and touch the wood of the piano. She said that if I kept my hands curved while I played and practiced, I could become a good piano player.

I followed what Sister Joseph Marie said. Now I played the piano with confidence. I thought about the hammer pins inside my piano. I thought of the different octaves and notes I played. I played hard. I obeyed the andante-slow and allegro-fast pace in the pieces before me.

I entertained myself by concentrating on the sheets of music in front of me. The sheets were held in place by an ornate piece of mahogany wood called the music desk. My fingers glided over the keys keeping me from distracted thoughts.

There was no discrimination between high or low octaves or the black or white keys. What mattered was the intensity of my play and the passion of my melody.

Diary Entry 59 - December 30

Today, I stretched my back out on the floor. I sat in the shower. I prayed the rosary. I rubbed my feet. I rubbed my tingling hands. I tried not to eat.

I was not good enough for me. I didn't know how to help myself. Age was winning. Satan was jumping on me and enjoying it.

Diary Entry 60 - January 6. Year Three.

I agreed to Speet's plan to try his hand and heart at music away from home. He beamed at my agreement. The plan was to move into an apartment with his friend who needed a roommate.

He would play his guitar and sing in different bars surrounding a nearby college campus. After a couple of months or more, Speet would decide to keep playing music at night, go back to school for a degree in music, or do both.

Today was the day that Speet set out on his own.

"How about some avocado toast before you leave?" I asked.

"Sure. Sounds good," Speet answered.

We looked at each other as we ate our toast.

We were at the front door. Speet had loaded his car earlier.

"Bye, Mom. I love you. Things will be great. I will call you. Keep in touch," Speet said.

"Goodbye, Speet. Take care of yourself. Call me whenever you can. I love you to the moon and back," I said.

I was happy for Speet. I prayed for his safety, happiness, and well-being. He said he would call when he could. I settled for that as we waved goodbye.

Off to Ms. Lee's office.

I sat in Ms. Lee's white, stark waiting room. There wasn't one print or painting on the walls. I criticized everything in the room. I knew why. I missed Speet.

Our meetings occupied days on my non-routine calendar. Even though we sat across from each other, most times I felt like a puppet on her lap and Ms. Lee was pulling my strings.

Did Ms. Lee have the intuitiveness and smarts to remove the thick wrapper around me? Self-mutilation was inside me. It was not the vomiting kind. It was the kind that intolerance and being enraged made you do. It was the kind that had your hands tied, your feet tied, your mouth taped, and your mind taken over. It was a self-kidnapping.

"Mrs. Patstegre, Ms. Lee is ready for you," the receptionist said.

I hurried up the right-angled staircases.

"Will Ms. Lee talk and leech out some of my cayenne blood?" I whispered out loud as I climbed.

"Hi, Ms. Lee," I said.

"Hi, Mrs. Patstegre. How have things been since we last talked?" Ms. Lee asked.

"Things have been fine. Listening to Cha Cha speak motivated me to write down tips that I use with Speet, Cha Cha, and others. I figured that some of my experience, awareness tips, language, and ideas might help other Caregivers," I said.

"Do you want to talk about any of them in particular?" Ms. Lee asked.

"Yes. Here are some that I wrote down that I find help most of the time. Nothing works all the time.

- o I free my mind and actions from negative thoughts and attitudes.

- o I do not move much when a loved one talks with me. I'm all-in.

- o I look into their eyes. I listen. I talk about what they want to talk about."

I took a drink of water.

"Please continue, Mrs. Patstegre."

"I will, Ms. Lee. Here is one I really like.

- o I use Tone Sharpening. Someone suffering from anxiety for example, may use sharp words with a hostile tone when talking. When I comment back to them, I don't use the same words that they used. I use my own words and sharpen my tone to the hostile sounding tone from their symptom-based words, that they used in their conversation with me. My hope is when they hear my copy-cat tone said back to them, it will cause them to pause before they continue their conversation with their same aggressive tone. Becoming mindful of their tone can calm the situation down."

"Mrs. Patstegre, using their tone is an interesting concept. Everyone always talks about the importance of listening. I imagine your tone concept might help," Ms. Lee said.

"I think it does. Most of the time after I use tone sharpening on them, their tone softens. Here are more tips that I use.

- o Mr. Patstegre used to say that we are on the same team. I use this phrase now.

- o I ask what I can do to make them feel safe.

- o I keep communication going in any form including texts, e-mails, in person, and the like. When my Mom died, I called my Dad every night for ten years. Some days, I was the only one he heard from all day.

- o I talk about positive attributes and talents of the person suffering.

- o I cook things they like when they come over.

- o I Don't Take Things to Heart - DTTH. If we have a heated conversation, I forget about hurtful words said. DTTH takes practice. It is not easy to train yourself to feel and act this way. It is a trait well worth learning, doing, and mastering to maintain good communication."

"Experience means a lot, Mrs. Patstegre. Like you said, nothing works all the time. Thank you for sharing your Caregiving skills and tips. Does it bring validation to how much you do?" Ms. Lee asked.

"I think it might. I believe I can always do more. However, there is only so much I can do," I answered.

"Can you repeat that last sentence, Mrs. Patstegre?" Ms. Lee asked.

I smiled. I knew what she was doing.

"There is only so much I can do," I answered.

"Let's stop here," Ms. Lee said.

"Bye, Ms. Lee. Thanks for today. See you soon."

Diary Entry 61 - January 9

Routines for me as a Caregiver consisted of grabbing a bag of chips, anything that was within reach, hair trained to look good without washing it every day, putting my hair on top on my head, brushing my teeth most nights, taking three-minute showers, and having toiletries packed for travel or trauma. Pre-packed items attracted my hands and my life.

Attention to how people looked, fit high on the scale of vanity. Vanity was an advantage to looks. Who didn't want to pamper themselves, have nice clothes, and look nice? I did. At the very least, I had a desire to self-care to feel better. Maybe that desire would expand to a must in the future for me.

Diary Entry 62 - January 11

God blessed me with the ability to fall asleep in many different places. I found a chair and the chair transformed to my body. The arms held me, and the chair said, "I will let you fall asleep fast, and I will pray that when you wake, I hurt, and your body doesn't."

Most of the time the chair was right.

Flexible sleeping habits helped during a crisis.

Diary Entry 63 - January 13

I was outside. I looked at all the leafless trees. Were they cold? I walked and nature talked. I wore a black wool coat and paired it with a black velvet, wide brimmed hat.

Every tree said something to me. Did other people pick up their sounds the way I did?

The leafless trees, as well as rain and snow, brought feeling to my life. Their curves, long reaching branch hands, broken bone branches, and their worn bark touched me.

Sometimes they waved and winked at me.

The top triangle toupees of pine needle trees were beautiful.

Nature didn't wear the latest style. Their bareness was their art.

Diary Entry 64 - January 18

I spoke to Speet over the weekend. Happiness voiced through the phone. We agreed that we would talk twice a month, even weekly if either one of us wanted to. It was nice to hear his voice.

I laid in bed. I geared myself up for a new cleaning job today.

Daisy and Effie had a friend whose husband had a fatal heart attack. They wanted me to help their friend by deep cleaning her house. What would I get out of this cleaning job? Doing a favor for them ended up being my reason for saying yes.

Vacky, my vacuum, Shiffty, my mop, and Minnet, my cleaning spray, and I showed up early at a house ridden with rugs of toys and mountains of clothes, a nightmare to a cleaner. Picking up clutter was not a part of a deep clean. I would have Vacky, Shiffty, and Minnet help with the mess.

"Oh, Cleaner Patstegre, I am at your command. I will propel myself and pick up these piles of clothes and toss them in the laundry room," said Shiffty.

Vacky chimed in, "I will toss the toys into the large baskets in the bedrooms."

"I will help you spray the dirtiest spots and leave everything shiny. I am Minnet at your service."

"We want you to author out your Caregiving knowledge, author out stormy stories, and author out your feelings. We will work fast so you can get home and write," Vacky, Shiffty, and Minnet said in unison.

"Thank you, troops. We are facing three bedrooms, two baths, and a hallway on the second floor. We have the staircase, a TV room, a living room, a half bath, and a kitchen on the first floor to clean. That's our project for today.

"Now that the clothes and the toys are picked up, let's start cleaning on the second floor. Minnet, let's start with you. Please note that it is nine o'clock in the morning and our goal is not the normal half day of cleaning. Let's shoot for an hour and a half. Minnet, let's get spraying and wiping," I said.

Help was glorious, if only in my imagination. The realness of my imagination made me whole.

Minnet sprayed the faucets with me. We wiped, quickly and firmly. We cleaned the sink. Minnet went up and down the neck of the sink. We squirted into lake twirl, wiped the rims, the seat, and the bird bath for butts. Now I brushed lake twirl and flushed.

Minnet sprayed the white tile and black and white checked border of the rain forest shower. The border reminded me of the borders on police hats in London. Minnet sparkled the tile and made the dirty grout in between disappear. I polished the chrome.

Now, on to the Jack and Jill, Jack and Jack, or Jill and Jill bathroom. Minnet and I cleaned it in the same fashion as the larger bathroom.

"Minnet, let's finish shining the chrome faucets and handles in this second bathroom. I'll spray, you wipe, Minnet. Done in record time," I said.

Shiffty stepped up behind me, almost tripping me.

"Reporting for duty," Shiffty said.

"Okay, Shiffty. Can you mop the floors while Minnet dusts the chest of draws and all the furniture in the bedrooms?" I asked.

"Sure," Shiffty answered.

Suddenly, Shiffty hit me on my arm and then on my back as I turned away. Had Shiffty flown into the air with me too many times and taken to hitting as a new profession?

"What the hell, Shiffty. Get off, get off," I said.

I had no idea why Shiffty would hit me like that. Was she thinking I was someone else? She seemed lost.

"Sorry about hitting you, Mrs. Patstegre. I am not myself today. I was daydreaming," Shiffty said.

"It's okay, Shiffty. I was a little shocked. You didn't hit me hard," I said.

"How time does not fly. It's still within two hours of starting and the dusting and the spraying are done on the second floor," I said.

Shiffty cleaned the wood floors around the rugs, under the beds, and around the furniture in record time. So much better than vacuuming the floors.

"Mrs. Patstegre, we are rounding the bend and finishing up the hallway, stairs, the bedrooms, and the bathrooms. We are on a fast track today," said Shiffty and Minnet.

Vacky hosed up.

"Now, my turn. I will peel up and down the rugs and take the outside layer off them. One for the money, two for the show, three to get ready and here's my hose," Vacky said.

We all went downstairs. Soon the carpets, floors, half-bath, kitchen, and furniture were clean on the first floor. Volant Vacky, Speedy Shiffty, and Meteoric Minnet had flown fast today.

The trifecta smiled at me, proud of themselves. They won me over with their hard work and their wanting to help me.

"Now you must write when we get home," said Vacky.

"We will put ourselves away," said Shiffty.

"Use your saved energy to write all afternoon," said Minnet.

"Thank you for all your help. I will explore my feelings on pages of comfort," I said.

The three screamed and jumped up and down with happiness. My short-term gratification of cleaning was shorter today. We did a kind deed. Would my authoring become long term gratification? Would I continue to write after *The Diary of a Caregiver* was finished? I hoped I would.

We drove home.

I ran into the house. I put Vacky, Shiffty, and Minnet down. They danced and yelled all the way to the pantry closet.

"Where are you, you new version of my beloved typewriter. Ah, there you are. Get ready for a ten-finger workout," I said.

My computer enjoyed watching and learning from someone who was not enamored with it. My computer wanted to know what made me tick; what made my ten-finger typing so rewarding. My computer wouldn't find out from me because it didn't feel, and right now, either did I. We had that in common.

Only my words projected scenes filled with meaningful colors.

Diary Entry 65 - January 19

I worked hard and long on writing yesterday. At the end of the day my computer ran slow and froze up.

This morning when my computer woke up it appeared fine. I wanted to call Thorndike, a tech expert who fixed my computer in the past. I had questions for him that I knew he could answer.

Thorndike fixed computers to help pay for his college degree in psychology.

Thorndike came to my house twice. Both times this superstar with his psychology and computer skills impressed me. Quiet and self-assured, Thorndike worked magic on my computer. When he worked, he fidgeted with his aviator glasses, occasionally twisting his blond ponytail.

"Hello," said Thorndike.

"Good morning, Thorndike. This is Mrs. Patstegre. You fixed my computer a couple of times. I thought it needed your mind and hands to fix it. However, my computer got better overnight.

"I still wanted to use your mind to get your opinion on something relating to the computer. I was curious about your thoughts on social media and psychological questions. It would be a brief conversation on the phone this morning. I will pay you your hourly rate," I said.

There was a pause. Thorndike barely knew me. Why would he take the time to talk with me?

"Thorndike, are you still there?" I asked.

"Sorry, Mrs. Patstegre, I lost my focus for a minute. Go ahead and ask your questions. Glad to help if I can," Thorndike answered.

"A couple of days ago, I had a conversation with a friend, Nelle, who determines how good or bad her day is by how many likes she gets on social media.

"She writes poetry. Many times, she puts her work on social media and waits for comments or likes. You have experience working and helping different people. You are young and interested in the human mind. What do you think of these lucky likes?" I asked.

"I don't like the heart like, thumbs up, slang, or icon thing they have on social media," Thorndike answered.

"After my friend, Nelle, put a poem on social media that she wrote, she did not get many likes. Her temperature of happiness went cold. What makes strangers' and acquaintances' opinions that important to people? People expose themselves on social media for connection and validation. Why can social media become the mood ring of the day for people?" I asked.

"Mood ring of the day is a good analogy, Mrs. Patstegre. It takes a thick skin not to be affected by the likes and negative comments. I don't think a confident person would pick social media to judge their work in the first place," Thorndike answered.

"I agree with your comments, Thorndike. Time evaporates quicker than boiling water when one is on social media. Drinking toward addiction, drugging toward addiction, and hearting toward addiction are all addictions.

"Thorndike, do you think social media encourages this seek-the-reward behavior?" I asked.

"I think so, Mrs. Patstegre. Maybe more people lack self-confidence than we realize. People may not see that their new connection in life may not be good for them. They should at least limit their time when they are on social media," Thorndike answered.

"Thanks for your insightful opinions, Thorndike. Good luck with school. I will send you a check for your time," I said.

"You are welcome. Mrs. Patstegre. No need for the check, glad to help."

We hung up.

Night fell upon me. I was in my bedroom. Talking Ceiling eye-balled me.

"Okay, Talking Ceiling. What's on your mind?"

"I heard you on the phone with Thorndike. Interesting conversation. I agree with both of you," Talking Ceiling said.

Talking Ceiling looked out for me. I was glad she thought the same as Thorndike and I felt about the superpower those social media likes and comments had over people.

Lying in bed, my mind drifted.

"Infinite highlights of red filters through my day. Fierceness slithers in my veins and arteries," I said.

"You must begin to feel, Mrs. Patstegre. It is the key to overcoming your fury and fears," Talking Ceiling pleaded.

"Maybe I am not ready to feel the heaviness of sadness from watching loved ones suffer," I said.

For a moment, I saw Talking Ceiling crack. Little hands emerged. They threw bolt shocks of touch at me.

"Ouch, stop it, are you really doing this to me?" I asked.

I found myself paralyzed on my back, unable to shield myself.

"I will help you start the process of feeling with seconds of bolts of shock. I will continue throwing them until you promise to start feeling on your own," Talking Ceiling said.

Talking Ceiling threw more shocks at me.

"Okay, okay, stop. Are you a Talking Ceiling and a Feeling Ceiling now? Did you have a conversation with Shiffty earlier? She threw a few hits at me in her supposedly dream like state. Was she trying to get me to feel too? I will try my best to start to feel," I said.

"That's all I am asking," Talking Ceiling said.

"Sleep don't haunt me tonight," I said.

I turned on my side, lifted my head and took a quick look upwards. I saw stillness, no little hands. I sighed, closed my eyes, and fell asleep.

Diary Entry 66 - January 21

Talking Ceiling irked me the other night with her shock touches. Although, she sent her shocks out of care, my blood pressure still spiked from getting hit by them.

I had an appointment with Ms. Lee today. I dragged myself in the shower, threw exercise clothes on, and wind dried my hair as I drove Bessie to Ms. Lee's office.

My annoyance flew me up the flights of right-angled stairs. Next thing I knew, I was sitting in our twin chairs to conversation.

"Why Mrs. Patstegre, you seem eager to talk. What is on your mind?" Ms. Lee asked.

"I am glad, I think, to be in your home away from home, office of talk therapy," I answered.

I looked at Ms. Lee for a reaction. There was none.

"The British are coming; the feelings are coming. This powerful outcry from Paul Revere and me are jump out of bed, catch the light, and feel more than what words allow," I said.

"Did something happen for you to bring up dialogue of this nature?" Ms. Lee asked.

Well, should I tell her my mop, named Shiffty, hit me to try and get me to feel even though I didn't know that was what she was doing? Should I also tell her that my Talking Ceiling threw shocks at me with her caring, white gloved hands pleading with me to feel on my own? I didn't think so.

"It doesn't matter, Ms. Lee. The details leading to the baking soda and vinegar outburst from me is not important. I am a paradox of what I see myself doing. I am a rocket blowing up but still reaching outer space. I am on an uncontrollable path with microscopic precision. I am everything and I am nothing.

"Is this Paul Revere outcry, my subconscious luring me out of emotional isolation, wanting me to start the process to recovery? Burying my feelings allowed me to function and be a good Caregiver.

"My co-morbid existence of surface facade for focus capability and my ignored sub-conscious is hurting me. I want more than survival and the ability to get things done. I'm confused, Ms. Lee," I said.

Ms. Lee pierced me with her eyes. Was she stunned, stupefied, or satisfied? I didn't care.

I didn't wait for her to say anything.

"Ms. Lee, I run with disgust and aggressiveness. I want to slow that run down," I said.

"What might you do to slow yourself down?" Ms. Lee asked.

Ms. Lee knew if she asked me too much, I might not return. She chose her words carefully and used few.

"I'm not sure. I know in my brain I must practice better self-care. I need to feel it in my heart," I answered.

"Is it possible to pause before you say yes to things?" Ms. Lee asked.

"I suppose I could try," I answered.

"Being a Caregiver is rewarding but stressful. Caregivers get worn out. You are here. That is a step to better self-care. Asking for help is a good thing. Caregivers need support, too," Ms. Lee said.

"Thank you, Ms. Lee. See you next time," I said.

Diary Entry 67 - February 4

I landed in Ms. Lee's office again. It was two weeks since I last saw her. She took a phone call, so I sat by myself. I noticed when I walked up the right-angle stairs leading to her office, that the steps had been cleaned. The carpet fibers stood up so straight. Did their vacuum get rid of the dirt in between the fibers? Would I stand up straight when I cleaned my brain, heart and body of my attitude, hate, and resentment?

I told myself to stop thinking so much as I sat in one of the matching unpredictable talk chairs.

Was my anger cracking after all these years?

Ms. Lee opened the door.

"Good morning. I'm sorry about the delay. It was an emergency call. I can add time to your next appointment," Ms. Lee said.

Ms. Lee sat down. A sliver of sunlight came through both sides of the drawn shades from the two windows in the room. Vitamin D rays from outside and dark lighting from inside caused gray mist within the room.

"Let's see where we end up today, shall we?" Ms. Lee asked.

I looked at this bright therapist wondering what her story was behind her degree. There was one. There always was. I decided for now, I didn't care to know the answer. To woo around the Mulberry Bush to get an answer would have to wait.

"Ms. Lee, stress hit me the other night as hard as a strong man hits his bell of height. I threw myself into a hot shower. The pressure from the water played patty-cake with my tension.

"Something inside is becoming uncontrollable and overwhelming. My dreams are trotting down paths that used to gallop. My body hurts. Connecting circuits of electricity increase my heart rate," I said.

I realized that Ms. Lee was listening to me. However, I was listening to myself more.

"Ms. Lee, sitting on the bench in my shower, I shivered through the steamy water. The horrible, devastating, scary, helplessness that people who suffer from severe mental illness can't be numbed by hot pellets of water.

"If you have never cared for someone that suffers from Bipolar, Schizophrenia, Clinical Depression, Post Traumatic Stress Disorder, an Eating Disorder, and/or Anxiety and Depression, then you can't fully understand what and how they feel. We as Caregivers have observed loved ones for decades. We suffer with them. They suffer more.

"Poor mental health robs people of reason, relationships, and consistent jobs, things that most people want," I concluded.

"I agree with everything you said. We have a minute or so left. Do you have any last thoughts?" Ms. Lee asked.

"No," I answered.

I left. I walked down the clean carpeted flights of stairs. On the last set of stairs, my hand let go of the rail and I jumped from the second step to the ground. My feet made a thud. People in the reception area looked up at me. I smiled and waved, not having any idea why I felt the need to jump off the last few steps.

Diary Entry 68 - February 7

My vocabulary was volcanic and vocalized in high pitches and low tones volleying for which direction my vice of violence and vindictiveness would go. Virgin vipers allowed my vice to become visceral.

Visions of vortexes were sent out to protect my loved ones, and suck in everything evil that got near them. Vulgar rhetoric and actions vied for attention as death fated its way into vertical and perpendicular grounding. I held vipers, one in each hand. I vectored where I needed to go to release the vipers.

All this vividness from constant visions of loved ones in pain.

Diary Entry 69 - February 8

I was frustrated by the judging notion from others that Caregiving was not a job. Caregiving was cap and gown, Ph.D. material. Not many saw that.

Diary Entry 70 - February 9

The imaginary aliveness of things and the fictional deserving of things allowed my feelings to be free.

The Cook, the Cleaner, the Mind Killer, the Client, and the Caregiver, had a talk on the top rung of my Ladder of Priorities. I was the main principal of myself. I asked them all to step down. I gave them the choice of going down one, two, or three rungs. They talked.

Cook and Cleaner decided it was their time to go down two rungs. Mind Killer decided it was time to go down three rungs. Client, the person seeking help, went down only one rung. The Caregiver stayed on the top rung.

"Mrs. Patstegre, go out to lunch and dinner, even breakfast more. It does not have to be expensive, just go," the Cook in me said.

"Mrs. Patstegre, let dust be a creative design in your house, let grime be a time of limitation. Let Vacky spare your shoulders. Let Shiffty and Minnet sweep and spray only the necessities," the Cleaner in me said.

"Keep searching for help, Mrs. Patstegre," the Client said.

Mind Killer remained silent, perhaps pouting, having gone down three rungs.

Cook, Cleaner, Mind Killer, and Client, all held me. The rungs of priorities changed today, even for Caregiving.

Caregiving for loved ones and Caregiving for myself were going to co-exist on the top rung.

Diary Entry 71 - February 15

"Talking Ceiling, are you there?" I asked.

"Yes, I am here," Talking Ceiling answered.

"Talking Ceiling, helpful words flow to my brain while caring for people. Mind Binders is the name I awarded to these spontaneous thoughts. Last time, before I knew you existed, I ran some Mind Binders by Speet. I wanted to see what he thought of them. Can I run this second set by you?" I asked.

"Absolutely, I would love to listen to your Mind Binders," Talking Ceiling answered.

"The Mind Binders are:

- o Mental illness is a bold thief. It steals in broad daylight and preys on the innocent. It does not need a getaway car. It's conceited enough to just walk away.

- o People bring in potted plants when they anticipate a frost. People cover young, fragile trees if there is a frost. Why don't people cover the homeless laying on the ground, especially when there is a frost?

- o Intravenous intuition is a pre-requisite for care.

- o Caregivers are master navigators of the wind. We know which direction to take when no one else does.

- o Caregivers wear a crown of a hundred jewels. Most of the time, they are the only ones who notice how rare these gems are and what they are worth.

    o   The blame-shame game is prevalent for couples that are Caregivers. We move the pieces on the board of living and take a card, saying you will have shame today or you will blame today."

"I like them all. The one about Caregivers and their crown of jewels is my favorite. I notice you. I know how much you do and how rare and real you are," Talking Ceiling said.

"Thank you for listening. I appreciate your kind words. I think you are great. Good night, Talking Ceiling," I said.

"Good night, sweet Mrs. Patstegre."

Diary Entry 72 - February 16

My imaginary ice cream cone was melting and so was the hard chocolate shell on top. It was dripping down the side of my cone to the floor. It reminded me of droplets of blood.

I was impatient in every direction.

"I am going against my proactive Caregiving nature. I am going to be reactive to my eagerness," I said out loud.

I grabbed my threat bag. I skipped around the house. I saluted to my jumping bean side of proactivity, who was napping tonight.

It was two o'clock in the morning. I couldn't wait to get out and yell or snarl at someone or something. I ran out the back door, a fraction off balance.

I was powerless to the nature around me.

I wasn't sure what was happening to me. Was I experiencing the circuits inside of me bumping into each other? Were my buried emotions melting from a deep freeze?

I must take full advantage of this defrosting. Why did I think advantage? Was this thawing really an advantage or was it a disadvantage to me? I didn't know.

My feelings appeared in Lady of Fatima style. No one else felt the intensity of them. No one else saw them.

I was a warrior of righteousness. I did not wick and whack the faithful or good. Oh no, I struck out at evil ones and mental health torturers. I was in a stab stance. My heart was high. I was in a violent vice. I howled out loud. I was now in the woods behind my house.

I saw a coyote. He was coy, skinny, and mean looking.

"You have no idea, little yowl, who you are looking at. I am part human and part animal. I am an emotional mutt. I am a combination of no conscience genes, high intelligence genes, strategic genes, and claw you to death genes.

"My claw paws are of invisible speed and blood curling nails. My yowl is higher pitched than a crying baby. I can twirl you around that tree, stretch your body until it is so paper thin that you will become a tree tattoo," I said.

I tamed smirking coyote with my rhetoric. He ran into the woods, afraid of me.

I looked around. I was rift rafting with my snot dripping cone of reaction. I stopped, not being able to control myself.

I took out the knife of knowledge from the threat bag and I just stabbed. I stabbed the ground so hard that the ground couldn't hold the blade. My strength lifted the blade out of the ground with buttery speed. I stabbed through leaves of blackness.

"I'm sorry leaves. I can't control my hand. Don't cut the roots, don't cut the roots. Let the plants out here live," I screamed.

"Hell no," another part of me said.

I was mad at everything and everyone. It was better than stabbing an Image of God person that lived down the lane, wasn't it?

I couldn't stop. I didn't want to. I dug to the roots. I beasted out some of the easier roots with my teeth, ate dirt and liked it. I stabbed, and stabbed, and stabbed, nicking myself here and near. I was out of breath, unable to see much. The moon was slivering in and out of the clouds. The darkness of the sky matched the values around me.

I dropped the knife into the open bag of threats and fell on my back. I laid there deep breathing. I shook my head. I messed up my hair. I smeared my bloody, muddy hands on my face. I flung dirt all over me.

"Should I sleep here?" I asked myself.

Without warning, a sweet, soft voice spoke.

"Oh, please don't stay here. You have village violated us. We have lived here for a long time. You come into our world and feel entitled to reveal your unrelenting anger on us. We saw and felt sorry for you. We watched your irate moves."

"Oh, sweet little voice, I can't see beyond the things that make me angry right now. I know not what I do," I said.

I felt hypnotized. This trance entranced me to go down a well of feeling.

It was the rule of recovery, I thought. I had a recovery room inside me that had a door to relief. The impulsive lack of control wanted the door to open, exposing buried emotions of unimaginable hurt from watching loved ones suffer from the horrid symptoms and thievery that backpacks on mental illness.

"I'm sorry village of nature," I said.

I got up, my head, my eyes, my heart looked at the ground. My feet moved in the direction of my backdoor.

My eyes opened. I was in my bed. My village that I invaded was a mind kill dream.

I gazed up at Talking Ceiling. She winked. I knew.

"Your shower awaits you, Mrs. Patstegre. Let the hot pellets of water melt away your stress. Did you dream? If yes, was your dream a mind killing one?" Talking Ceiling asked.

"Yes and no. I ruffled up plants, weeds, and leaves. I think I replaced the ones I tore up so they wouldn't die. I can't remember. It was a mind hurt dream responding to spontaneous irritation rather than a mind kill," I answered.

I slipped into my shower of snugness, snagged the relaxation bench, baked in warm water, and told myself it would all be okay.

Diary Entry 73 - February 18

I, Mrs. Patstegre, existed in a fictional or real fashion in everyone. Who hadn't had pain or trauma? How many people acted out in agony in a kaleidoscope fashion? Actions were different every time you moved the pieces.

I lived with elements inside of me. They helped me throughout my day. I chose three elements to help me. One was Helium. She was noble. Her clean clarity lifted me up when I needed it.

Uranium was my fighter. She bent, flipped, and cooked into action if needed. She was my weapon, with 92 rounds of Proton Protection and 92 rounds of Electron Electricity. She fired with intuition.

Finally, there was Aluminum. She walked and talked with me. She had a great liking toward oxygen. She held my hand and helped me deep breathe when anxiety was high and daily rhythms were disrupted.

Did I need instrumental vision to navigate through the Nantucket fog that lived with me in my imaginary recovery room? In my recovery room, deep feelings were tamed by unreal numbing drips of morphine, so that life could go on.

Diary Entry 74 - February 19

I arrived early to Hookum Soup Kitchen.

I was a private person. My woo-ness to the truth knew that Gus's cricketing around me was his way of attempting to unlock my brain.

He was a worm of opportunity that made me want to peck at him. His slim yet connecting intuitive mind could expose me. Expose what though? He could dig around with his snoopy nose and find out things about Speet's trauma and our personal life. He couldn't find out about my mind kills; they weren't real.

Gus was trying to finish an amputated education. He said the soup kitchen work was for extra credit to get a better grade. Was that a lie?

Maybe Gus was completing his degree, but he failed to tell me that he also worked as a private investigator or police officer. Ms. File at Concerned Nursing confided those facts to me.

I envisioned a smoking red halo floating over Gus's head.

I took a couple of deep breaths.

"There you go, letting your rhetoric get the best of you. Aggravation can scale high with extreme written or spoken words. Imaginary thoughts become hot with protective Caregiving," I muttered to myself.

A loud thud interrupted my thoughts. Gus had arrived, letting the door slam behind him.

"Hi, Gus. I'll wrap forks inside napkins and put them on the little round table in the corner of the dining hall. Can you put the tablecloths on the long, rectangular tables for our guests?" I asked.

"Sure. There are some plants that someone has been watering in the other room. I will put those on the tables," Gus answered.

"Good idea, Gus. So many of the homeless that come into the soup kitchen had nice things in their previous lives. They fell on bad luck, bad situations, and bad illnesses. Niceties in any fashion show respect.

"The homeless deserve a caring look into their eyes, not an up and down glance that snobby women and men do to make themselves feel better," I said.

"Lady Patstegre, you are hard to figure out. You have manners like a lady, yet there is something mysterious about you," Gus said.

"Gus, I zig-zag through life the best I can. My mysterious air that you say I carry is because Caregivers must have a flare for the fire that glows in, out, all around loved ones that suffer from mental illness," I said.

Did I tell him too much about me and Caregiving? Would he ask me who I cared for? He probably thought I was talking about the homeless. I still needed to be careful. He smelt and saw things that others didn't.

I pulled the pans of lasagna out of the ovens. I filled bowls with lovely green salad. I cut French bread and put it in baskets I brought with me to Hookum.

"Gus, please put the bread baskets on the tables. You know the drill," I said.

"Sure, Lady Patstegre. I know you hate me calling you that name. The title fits you though," Gus said.

Our full capacity crowd left. I wished I could offer hot showers and heaters of warmth to all our homeless that we served at Hookum.

Gus and I cleaned up after serving over one hundred homeless people.

Gus helped me take the empty lasagna pans and the rest of my things to Bessie.

We left the soup kitchen and went our separate ways.

Diary Entry 75 - February 20

Ms. Lee caught a virus. She had been home sick for a week or so. The phone rang. It was the receptionist from Ms. Lee's office. Ms. Lee decided to come into work, even though it was a Saturday. The receptionist wanted to know if I would like a session today at ten o'clock. I thanked her for calling me and said that I would be there. I figured Ms. Lee must be on the mend.

It was nine o'clock in the morning. I drove fast. Bessie and I listened to music. Bessie started to sing. When she sang, she moved her silver grate in front of her hood, ever so slightly. Then she moved one eye headlight up and the other down at the same time.

"You are my piccadilly pride, Bessie. Lead the way to our place of spoken words. It is the feeling part that quicksands my five stages of grief. Ms. Lee wants to start pulling up some of that grief," I said.

I jumped out of Bessie. I was early. Ms. Lee was in the waiting area. We walked up the stairs to our chairs of communication.

"Good morning, Ms. Lee. I'm glad you are feeling better," I said.

"Thank you, Mrs. Patstegre. How are you doing?" Ms. Lee asked.

I stared at Ms. Lee. She stared back.

Was her question more of a feeling question instead of a doing question? I chose to ignore it.

I rolled my eyes everywhere in my body except where she could see them. My acrobatic jubilee answered, "Binge eating is a past time of negativity."

"Mrs. Patstegre, please expand on that concept," Ms. Lee said.

"Ms. Lee, stress forces my hand to grab food and eat it. I'm not hungry for food. I'm hungry for relief," I said.

"It is hard to stop stress eating. We can work on ways that would help you stop. Please continue with your thoughts," Ms. Lee said.

"Negative hypnotic nightmares flash unwanted commercial reminders of anger. How many times do we change the channels on the television when commercials appear? Nightmares don't allow one to change the course it's supposed to take," I said.

"Can you tell me more, Mrs. Patstegre," Ms. Lee asked.

"No. I'm tired, Ms. Lee. I know I have more time. I need to be somewhere by eleven," I answered.

"That's fine. See you soon," Ms. Lee said.

"Thanks, Ms. Lee."

As I walked to Bessie, I felt an electric fraying in my body. I embraced her steering wheel and closed the door. I took some deep breaths. My unraveling decreased.

"Let's drive, Bessie. You are the only tranquilizer that I can legally drive on," I said.

Diary Entry 76 - February 22

I covered my emotions better than the best wallpaperer. Was that a word? Don't care, it worked. Recently, the corners of my wallpaper started to fray and disconnect. Bad wiring was being discovered. My ripped corners, like my clothes, were like corners of furniture chewed by a puppy, and old like my body, my skin, my hair, and my strength. My exposed wallpaper was not pretty like the wallpaper on one's computer.

Exposure reduced my strength and my support beams. Exposure weakened me. Exposure diminished being affective and effective.

Diary Entry 77 - February 23

I witnessed creative power from those that suffered from mental illness, trauma, and abuse.

Anxiety, depression, and the symptom spectrum of mental illness eventually cooked a fine sugar, a sweetness filled with determination that was breathtaking to watch.

The intensity, the mind holding, the triggers and symptoms, the words and music felt by those that suffer from mental pain was a rainbow of color. Nourished creativity soothed the pain side of that rainbow allowing a path for their genius/creative power to surface.

This was what I witnessed. This was what I saw. This was what I believed.

Diary Entry 78 - February 24

"Talking Ceiling, are you there? I have another set of Mind Binders that I would like to run by you," I said.

"I am here. I would love to hear your Mind Binders," Talking Ceiling said.

"Thank you, Talking Ceiling. I appreciate it. Here they are:

- o Caregivers, invisible to most, noticeable to God, go to Heaven because they give so much that they slide through the eye of the needle.

- o You are not the illness. The illness is the illness. You have symptoms of the illness that you are carrying. You are you. You are precious. You are the only you.

o   The protective nature of the brain is amazing.

o   We need defibrillators and pacemakers for regulation of moods.

o   You do not know if a roof is leaking until you live under it.

o   People polish things, many times forgetting to buff things out."

"I like all of them, especially the second one. Keep writing and sharing your Mind Binders," Talking Ceiling said.

Diary Entry 79 - February 26

Ms. Lee ended up having surgery. Her office presented me with names of several therapists with different levels of education that could take her place. I reached out to Dr. Tantrum, a psychiatrist.

Today, I had my first appointment with him.

I sat in the parking lot adjacent to Dr. Tantrum's office. His office was in a two story, rectangular building. The outside of the building wore a coat of white, rough stucco. Two glass doors at the front entrance reminded me of flippers on a pin-ball machine. Those flippers pushed all the hesitant people into the offices of watering eyes that were supposed to make people feel better.

I walked down the hall to Suite 13B. There were four engraved brass plaques screwed on a white painted door. Dr. Tantrum, Psychiatrist, was engraved on one of those plaques. I pushed the door open. I went into the waiting room.

A man talking with a woman behind small, sliding glass windows, eyed, and smiled at me. I assumed the man was Dr. Tantrum and the woman was his assistant.

The man walked away.

The assistant slid open one of the windows.

"Are you Mrs. Patstegre?" she asked.

"Yes, I am," I answered.

"Please take a seat, Mrs. Patstegre. Dr. Tantrum will be right out."

In a couple of minutes, a door opened in a hallway, not far from me. A tall man, the one I concluded was Dr. Tantrum, approached me.

"Mrs. Patstegre, I am Dr. Tantrum.

Dr. Tantrum was an older man with gray and brown layers of hair. His eyes were surrounded by tortoiseshell glasses. He wore a white button-down collar shirt and blue jeans. His camouflage outfit shouted out an air of trust and down to earthiness. Was he really like that?

Did Dr. Tantrum possess hefty bags of tools to unwind me, unscrew me, remove the nails from me, or sandpaper me?

Was he extra-ordinary to remove scars on my outer frame to gain insight?

Was he eyeing me? Was I eyeing him? Of course.

I sat in a leather chair in Dr. Tantrum's modern office of distinction.

The wood arms on the chair looked like paddles on ceiling fans. Ceiling fans nauseated me. They made the room spin.

"Dr. Tantrum, may I sit on the sofa, instead of this chair?" I asked.

"Of course," Dr. Tantrum answered.

I moved to the bigger sofa. The two paddle arms grabbed at me, at least it seemed like that. I wondered if the good doctor noticed that. I didn't care. I wanted answers to my questions.

Dr. Tantrum studied me from his desk chair. I didn't blame him. I aspired to correctness, why wouldn't he?

I taught myself to swim, learned to read tides, understood the danger of currents, knew when a squall was coming, and knew the smell of snow. I was a self-taught weather person, a fine-tuned predictor.

Dr. Tantrum, at present, wasn't ever going to get my armor off completely. Never. Even in Care Heaven, I envisioned my armor existing underneath a beautiful robe of softness just in case anyone needed me on Earth. I believed I would be able to woo God into letting me go for a care visit.

A silent conversation persisted for a while.

Dr. Tantrum wheeled his desk chair closer to me and sat down across from me. He looked at my body language, placement of my hands, and my slightest movements. I did the same.

Did he hear my conversation with myself? What section of the DSM, Diagnostic and Statistical Manual, the bible of diagnostic codes and diagnoses in the Psychiatry world, fit me? None of them. There wasn't a code for what a Caregiving's life was, at least I didn't think so.

Silence continued. We hit a silent ball back and forth until it became as big and as hard as a basketball. I decided to make a basket. I said to myself that I had won. I made the basket, but did the coach get more insight into me than I wanted him to see? Did he find things out from my silence and imaginary thoughts?

I broke the quietness and spoke.

"Bench-pressing strength circulates through my mind to get through my day. Lack of tears provide immeasurable energy to me. You could say that I am in the best mental condition in my life, toned to perfection. Experience, intuition, and true woo frame me. I fly forward in the Caregiving direction I need and want to go. This is why I am here," I said.

"I am glad you are here," Dr. Tantrum said.

I was nervous. I needed fresh air. I knew I was only there a short amount of time.

"I am finished for today. Thank you. It was nice to meet you," I said.

"May I use the Ladies room?" I asked.

"The bathroom is down the hall, first door on your left," he answered.

I sprinted to the large door marked Women. I splashed water on my face. Looking in the mirror, I hung on to the sink for support, shook my head, and sent myself out of the bathroom and out of the all-seeing doors of psychiatry.

My first meeting with Dr. Tantrum made me wonder if he might be rare enough, time available enough, and smart enough to help me. At least, death to the psychiatrist on first sight did not happen.

Diary Entry 80 - February 27

I had lunch with Cha Cha today at Jacks, a favorite diner of mine. Jacks had round red leather stools at the counter. Good old fashioned, comfort food was served twenty-four hours a day. Some employees had worked at Jack's for over twenty years.

Cha Cha and I sat at a table covered with a red and white checked tablecloth, silverware, and a black and chrome napkin holder. The paper napkins sprung in on both sides.

"You know Mrs. Patstegre, I wish I knew why my anxiety races at times. The deep breathing techniques that you taught me really help. I use coping skills to calm myself. I still wish I knew the reason why I get these fearful and out of control feelings," Cha Cha said.

"Cha Cha, I read an article titled, 'My Anxiety Makes My Brain Feel Like a Broken Hamster Wheel', by Mary Ladd and medically reviewed by Dillon Browne, Ph.D. I copied some points in her article on my phone. May I read them to you?" I asked.

"Sure," Cha Cha answered.

"Mary Ladd said, 'Anxiety is my body's way of responding to stress. It's the exact opposite of calm. Having anxiety is a normal part of life, but when I don't process stress in a healthy way, my brain keeps churning day and night. And when the symptoms take over, I feel like a hamster running in a wheel,'" I said.

"That's how I feel sometimes," Cha Cha said.

"In her article, Ladd said that there were five indicators that allowed one to know if their anxiety was accelerating to intense fear and panic. According to Ladd, the five indicators are:

'1. Obsession or an endless thought loop that leaves you exhausted.
2. Avoidance or ignoring what you need.
3. Overplanning or trying to control the uncontrollable.
4. Restlessness or not being able to sleep.
5. Traces of deteriorating physical health,'" I said.

Cha Cha nodded at me to continue.

"Ladd also said, 'The more I get tired, the more I ponder a million details per minute. This inability to rest and stop worrying can be a giant sign that things are out of control. Perhaps I'm trying to crowd out my own thoughts and emotions by thinking about others. This helps me avoid things that perhaps are too painful to face, acknowledge, or process,'" I said.

I decided to quote Mary Ladd's exact words to Cha Cha because I liked the way she described her anxiety in her article.

"Her words make sense. I need to pay better attention to these indicators. Can you please email them to me?" Cha Cha asked.

"Of course, Cha Cha," I answered.

"Thank you, Mrs. Patstegre," Cha Cha said.

"Cha Cha, worrying too much about others and other things, makes you not deal with your core feelings, triggers, and symptoms. Fear and panic can take over. Removing yourself from the worrisome situation, proper breathing, and winding down can prevent fear from going into the fight and flight mode," I said.

Cha Cha and I continued to teeter-totter talk. Warmness and welcomeness made our meetings meaningful.

Cha Cha had to run to a meeting. We hugged. I told Cha Cha it was my treat for lunch. Off she went.

I stayed to finish my coffee. As I sipped my coffee, I noticed a young boy at the table next to me, maybe eighteen years of age, with a glass of water in front of him. The waitress was asking if she could take his order. He shook his head no.

She looked upset. He looked sad.

I knew that the waitress preferred to have paying customers at one of her tables, rather than a water drinker.

Did the boy with the glass of water want food but didn't have money to pay for it? Was he angry that he was hungry and he couldn't afford to eat? Did he want help?

I overheard the waitress unload her frustration to her manager over the boy not ordering food. The manager nodded her head toward the waitress acknowledging her aggravation.

The waitress walked toward the boy.

"I talked with my manager. Unless you order some food, we would like you to leave so the table is free for paying customers," the waitress said to the boy.

The boy looked at her. He didn't talk. He held his hands together on the table for control. He looked upset and fearful to me. Was he going to create a scene?

The waitress uttered words under her annoyed breath as she walked away. I understood her. I felt sorry for her and the boy.

I wanted to say something to the boy looking at his glass of water. I pondered what words I should start off with. My instincts lead me to his feet. He wore nice looking tennis shoes. They appeared new. I liked them. My words would be an honest complement.

"I like your white, high top tennis shoes. They look new. Are they?" I asked.

He stunned stared at me.

"Yes, they're new," he answered.

"Are they your favorite shoes?" I asked.

"Kind of. I spent most of my paycheck on them. I shouldn't have but I did. I wish I could take them back. I can't," he answered.

I smiled.

His lips smiled back. His eyes looked worried.

"I have a son who likes his shoes made from man-made materials instead of leather. In other words, he prefers vegan shoes as well as vegan food," I said.

"I'm sure in some restaurants getting vegan food might be a problem," he said.

"Speaking of a problem in a restaurant, I see that you are drinking water and you have been here for a while. May I buy you a sandwich and some fries or something else on the menu?" I asked.

He tilted his head trying to figure out if I was a good witch or a bad witch.

"Yes, I will take a cheeseburger and fries to go," he answered.

"Okay. I'll let your waitress know to place the order," I said.

I walked to where the waitress was standing. Her name tag spelled Maisie. She looked fifty something. She wore her hair in a bun and was an attractive lady.

Some of the regular waitresses wanted to retire in the next year or two. I noticed Jacks was training a couple of new ones. Maisie was one of the trainees.

"Excuse me, Maisie. I would like to buy the young man with the glass of water a cheeseburger and an order of fries to go. Please add it to my bill," I said.

"I will. It's nice of you to buy him food. Thanks for helping him and calming my frustration," Maisie said.

I walked back to my table.

"I put your order in. It shouldn't take long. I'm Mrs. Patstegre. What is your name?" I asked.

"My name is Wilbur," he answered.

"Well, Wilbur, it is nice to meet you," I said.

We talked to each other, table to table, person to person. It was nice.

I looked up. I saw Maisie walking toward us.

"Here is your order to go. Have a wonderful day," Maisie said.

Wilbur got up, looked at me, said thanks, and walked to the door. He looked back and gave a slight wave to me.

I waved back.

I took several ice cubes from my glass of water and dropped them into my cup of coffee. I felt like ice coffee. I felt a little warm.

Did a cheeseburger and fries fuel down a fire that could have escalated next to me?

I saw and heard Wilbur. Many people didn't take the time to wear the shoes of others and feel the meaning behind their words. Watching eyes, hand movements, the need for attention and care, and the longing desire for help was a must to understand the awkward outward behavior exhibited at times by others.

I guessed that Wilbur was hungry and wanted something to eat, but discovered he didn't have money in his pocket. Was he too embarrassed to tell Maisie? Maybe. I knew that he did not know what to do.

I finished my ice coffee. Maisie came over. I paid my bill and gave her a large tip.

"You know, I saw the boy you bought lunch for go to a bench across the street where a younger boy sat. Maybe it was his brother. Anyway, they both ate the food you bought. I just thought you might want to know," Maisie said.

"Thanks, Maisie. I think I'll sit here for a minute or two. Is that okay?" I asked.

"Sure, stay as long as you want," Maisie answered.

I thought about how Maisie's frustration and Wilbur's anxiety confronted each other today.

Wilbur, like many other people who needed food, money, and necessities, worried about everything. Wilbur on top of being hungry, probably felt guilty about buying his new tennis shoes. His sensitivity and anxiety rounded into a ball of emotions.

In today's case with Wilbur, I caught the ball of his sensitivity and anxiety before the bounces encouraged irrational thinking. In his heightened state of anxiety, Wilbur might have misunderstood Maisie's frustration for bossiness and unkindness.

Wilbur couldn't see his sensitivity zapping rational thinking. He missed the signs and clues around him.

I used patience, intuition, a helping heart, and connecting eyes to help Wilbur trust me. A scene brooded over a glass of water and unknown circumstances. A peaceful solution was accomplished with a cheeseburger and fries.

I walked out of Jacks. The sun hit the backs of the two boys walking down the street. A twinkle tickle shivered goosebumps inside of me on this non-raining, feeling kind of day.

Diary Entry 81 - February 28

I laid on my bed watching episodes of an old TV series called *The Legend of Wyatt Earp*. In the series, Wyatt Earp, a Marshal for the United States, Doc Holiday, Wyatt's friend and supporter, and Shotgun, one of Wyatt's deputies, defended the innocent and conquered evil. For me, the series created a thought free space away from anger. Relaxing my anger was rare. The Wyatt Earp series de-stressed me.

"Mrs. Patstegre, I have been watching the series with you. I believe these men have a calming effect on me, too. I am excited to watch more episodes with you," Talking Ceiling said.

"Before we watch more episodes, would you mind listening to a few more Mind Binders I came up with?" I asked.

"Go ahead, Mrs. Patstegre. I'm listening," Talking Ceiling answered.

"There are five of them. Here they are:

o   Movement prevents mind muck.

o   If you need clarity, wash a window. It helps.

o   Reactive symptom words sound like instruments in an orchestra, out of tune, off beat, and off pitch. DDTH - Don't Take Things to Heart helps desensitize a situation. Things then become more in tune.

o   A stop sign of symptoms can pop up anytime and force loved ones who suffer from mental illness to slow their pace in life. Missing out on things that others take for granted becomes commonplace.

o   Masks worn on the outside makes one wonder how many masks are worn on the inside."

"I like all five. Now let's get back to watching *The Legend of Wyatt Earp*," Talking Ceiling said.

I laughed.

"Okay, Talking Ceiling," I said.

Diary Entry 82 - March 1

I stared at the building of hard edges that housed Dr. Tantrum's office.

A cancellation allowed me to see him sooner than later.

His smart intuition told me he would answer my questions with conviction and knowledge. His mannerisms backed up that assumption.

How much experience did he have? How much experience evolved from Caregiving for a loved one that suffered from any form of mental illness versus medical school requirements?

As a Caregiver I wanted advice and help to better take care of myself.

Caring for others took eight cylinders of power to forge ahead.

Cowardness was extinct. Intuition prevailed. Quitting was not a card game that I played.

I was late. I jumped out of Bessie, closed her door, and ran into Dr. Tantrum territory. He was waiting for me outside his office, in the waiting room.

"I'm sorry I am late," I said.

"It's not a problem," Dr. Tantrum said.

I sat down in Dr. Tantrum's room of clarity and cleanliness. My eyes and mood were slightly brighter for this second meeting of our minds.

"How have you been since our first meeting?" Dr. Tantrum asked.

"I have been fine," I answered.

"Why don't you lead the conversation, Mrs. Patstegre," Dr. Tantrum said.

I paused and thought. Should I reveal my mind kill charm on my make-believe charm bracelet? Did he think that I would divulge other charms dangling from my wrist?

Dr. Tantrum nodded to proceed.

"As a Caregiver, I put patience on the front burner, many times on high heat. I revolve like a Ferris wheel, going round and round with few stops.

"I hold people in my arms physically and mentally with my Caregiving love and words. Some say that I ease the habitual circle of pain and trauma by letting them know I am there for them. A Caregiver is on call twenty-four hours. I'm longing for carving time in those twenty-four hours for self-care," I said.

"Self-care is important. Mrs. Patstegre, your words warrant my admiration and attention," Dr. Tantrum said.

"I need to grab and accept idleness. I want to teach myself how to welcome self-thoughts, self-circles, and self-necessities. I want enough self-care to achieve respect for myself. Does that make sense, Dr. Tantrum?" I asked.

"Yes, it does. We can work on ways to reach your goal of self-care," Dr. Tantrum answered.

"Thank you. I sense a stop sign rising inside of me. I will stay longer next time we meet. Slowness in this situation speaks success to me. Instinct inserts that idea. I believe a sun peeking in and out of the clouds is the pace that will melt my ice-mold of controlled feelings," I said.

"Okay, Mrs. Patstegre. I will see you soon," Dr. Tantrum said.

As I walked toward Bessie, I looked behind me and saw Dr. Tantrum looking sideways out his window into woods next to his building. What was he staring at? It didn't look like anything specific.

Diary Entry 83 - March 3

Day turned to night with little physical movement from me.

Overwhelming tiredness made me jittery and sleepy. I rested in my bed.

"Talking Ceiling, do you want to know how my appointment was with Dr. Tantrum the other day?" I asked.

Her eyes appeared and opened.

"Yes, please tell me," Talking Ceiling answered.

"I could be wrong, Talking Ceiling, but I envision Dr. Tantrum aiding me in my journey of discovery. This isn't going to be a gut course to success. It will be a challenging course like an advanced statistics course in psychology," I said.

"I hope that Dr. Tantrum pulls through for you, Mrs. Patstegre," Talking Ceiling said.

"I hope so, too," I said.

I decided to write in my diary. I wanted my wings of prickly anger to fly any direction it wanted, allowing my words to surprise me.

"I'll watch over you while you write," Talking Ceiling said.

"Thanks, Talking Ceiling."

Diary Entry 84 - March 8

"Good morning, Mrs. Patstegre," Dr. Tantrum said.

"Good morning, Dr. Tantrum," I said.

"Last time we were together, you talked about being a Caregiver and searching for ways to have more time for yourself. Would you like to start today by talking about Caregiving in general or skills that you have developed?" Dr. Tantrum asked.

Oh, he was smart. He suspected that my skills could be talked about because of my experience. They were easy to talk about. My feelings were not. Dr. Tantrum hoped that my skills might London Bridge to openness. He didn't ask about my feelings because he knew I would have deer jumped in front of his headlights, sped to the woods, and be gone forever from sight.

"Okay, I will talk about my Caregiving life," I answered.

Dr. Tantrum warmed a smile and a nod my way. I refrained from looking at Dr. Tantrum. Then I thought, I should peek to see how much he was or wasn't listening to me. When I looked up, he sat still.

Dr. Tantrum's statue-like body paid attention to me. Respect shown from him earned more words spoken from me. It became evident that Dr. Tantrum desired me to continue, with no interference from him. So far, so good.

"I graze daily in a refrigerator filled with ice coffee and sandwiches with easy and non-healthy ingredients. Stocked in my kitchen are attractive, safe, easy to grab food.

"Recently, an inchworm is creeping around me and encouraging me to fly and grab sandwiches and food with healthy ingredients," I said.

Once again, I looked up. He sat even more statue-like if that was possible. He played his hand well. He had good insight.

"Dr. Tantrum, I Don't Take Things to Heart most of the time. I refer to it as DTTH. Harsh words and actions said from irritability, anger, and restlessness, symptoms of anxiety and other mental illnesses, are said from pain. I know the harsh words are not directed at me. I try to care with grace, kindness, and complementary words and actions," I said.

"Wonderful insight. Beautiful words. Please continue, Mrs. Patstegre," Dr. Tantrum said.

"DTTH - Don't Take Thing to Heart, are bricks to further togetherness. The more you DTTH, the higher the bricks are laid. Strong bonds are built. This closeness changes with age and situations, but once built, the foundation lasts," I said.

"Please go on, Mrs. Patstegre," Dr. Tantrum said.

"The earth is round and so is our life. When you are born, you are at the beginning of your roundness. You rely on Caregivers. As years of living increase, and the circle of roundness turns, Caregivers will need care. We will all end up needing care. Thus, the roundness of life and care continues," I concluded.

I took a breath. I thought of Clippy. The roundness worked for friendship, too.

"Mrs. Patstegre, you paused," Dr. Tantrum said.

"Sorry, Dr. Tantrum. I am fine. My mind thoughts wanted attention," I said.

"I think I want to stop talking. Thank you, Dr. Tantrum, for your Lincoln Memorial pose. I will be back. I might want to try a phone conversation for ease next time," I said.

"I prefer for now, that you come in unless you are sick," Dr. Tantrum said.

"Okay, I will see you in person," I said.

"Goodbye, Mrs. Patstegre," Dr. Tantrum said.

"Goodbye, Dr. Tantrum. Have a nice day," I said.

As I walked to the car, I looked up and saw Dr. Tantrum looking out the window like last time. He looked like he was stretching out his back.

I was glad Dr. Tantrum was prepared for our session. He listened well. I needed him to teach me a better strategy for living and caring for myself for the future.

But how was Dr. Tantrum going to teach me something so foreign to me?

I needed help with the constant deciphering of what level help a loved one needed and what was necessary, wanted, implied, unsaid, up in the air, and/or just damn unknown.

What did levelness and evenness in Caregiving look like? How was the pie of Caregiving and Self-Care sliced? How often did that change and did it/should it only change due to emergencies and crisis?

Did I even believe the words that I just wrote? This was hard and perplexing to me in a masterful way. How could I put myself above caring for others unless physical limitations rendered me powerless? I did not know the answer.

I sat on my bed thinking.

Talking Ceiling made her presence known.

"Hi, Mrs. Patstegre. How was your appointment with Dr.Tantrum?" Talking Ceiling asked.

"It went well. I think Dr. Tantrum can help," I answered.

"I'm glad," Talking Ceiling said.

"There is an uncontrollable green light pushing me to discover myself. The question is, how many emotions do I want to uncover? Half the time I think feeling and acknowledging buried emotions will kill me, paralyze me, or God knows what to me," I said.

"You are thinking too much. Please try and sleep now," Talking Ceiling said.

"I'll try. Good night, Talking Ceiling. Thanks for listening," I said.

"I will always listen to you. Good night, Mrs. Patstegre."

I laid in bed still thinking. My muse, Talking Ceiling, although made-up, was blissful company.

Diary Entry 85 - March 9

Privacy allowed my intenseness to squint out words of release.

Sidetracked meanings were driven by my inner emotions, not spoken, or consciously felt. Remarks nerve celled from my mind into my writing.

I hoped my words connected to other Caregivers. I aspired for all ages to connect with the words in *The Diary of a Caregiver* and nurture a better understanding of the pain and stigma associated with caring for those with mental illness.

Diary Entry 86 - March 10

"My dear Talking Ceiling, an episode of mental illness is the same thing as a stroke and a heart attack. All need medical care and transportation to a place that can help. Do all agree with that? They should. Some don't.

"Many times, rehabilitation is recommended after surgery. It is covered by insurance companies for physical problems. Most times, long term rehabilitation is recommended following an episode of psychosis from mental illness but is not covered by insurance.

"Usually only short term, acute care is covered. Family members, the ones that understand the need for care, cover long-term care of a loved one suffering after acute care by providing support, housing, transportation, care, and money.

"The brain is an organ as is the heart. Where is the fairness in care? There is none," I said.

"I know Mrs. Patstegre, I know," Talking Ceiling said.

Diary Entry 87 - March 11

The Love Dos were written with Speet in mind to help with daily rhythms and to promote good habits and self-care.

Sister Therese of Lisieux said, "Remember nothing is small in the eyes of God. Do all that you do with love."

Love Dos were not meant to be overwhelming; they were meant to be loving. They could be personalized.

I stood up from my desk of support. I decided to read the Love Dos out loud to hear how they sounded.

"The Love Dos Are:

<u>Daily Rise</u>
Get up within an hour of what your alarm is set to? Better yet, can you get up within fifteen minutes of what your alarm is set to? It's your life, you know how much time it takes for you to get up.

<u>Daily Breakfast and Nutrition</u>
Eat something, a protein bar, toast, fruit, something to get you started in the morning.

<u>Daily Care of Self</u>
Take a shower or bath. Give yourself hugs for the day. If you are working at home, brush or comb your hair. Put comfortable clothes on. Brush your teeth.

<u>Daily Activation of Work/Volunteer Work</u>
Being prepared for your job or a volunteer position is a prudent thing to do. You know yourself best. You know how much time you need to get ready. Plan accordingly. This can be tough and may have to be practiced.

<u>Daily Spiritual Nutrition And Mindfulness</u>
This can be any kind of spiritual mindfulness that you want. Be mindful of your surroundings and evidence of the truth. Take a moment to rub out the devil's tattoo of negative thoughts.

<u>Daily Deep Breathing</u>
Deep breathing a couple of times brings relief from anxiety. Breathe through your nose. Breathe in and up through your chest, pushing your stomach out. Breathe out slowly

through your nose, pulling your stomach in as far back as you can, trying to touch your belly button to your back.

Daily Picturing Yourself Doing Something
If life gives you a dreadful day filled with anxiety, depression, or both, it is hard to do much of anything. This Love Do says if you can picture yourself making a sandwich, taking a shower, walking around your place, doing something, you might begin to feel like doing it. Imagining it might be the push needed to make movement happen.

Daily Ping-Pong Communication
Back and forth dialogue with someone is an old-fashioned way of relieving stress. Take a moment and talk with someone.

Daily Lunch
Love yourself and eat something for lunch. Call and ask for someone to bring you food if you need to.

Daily Rustle-Bustle Cleaning
Cleaning can be short term gratification. It's magic muscle movement.

Daily Click-Clock Exercise
Walk around your place or outside if you can manage it. Do stretching exercises or more strenuous exercising if you can. It is up to you. Dance around to music.

Daily Break-a-Leg Performance
Play an instrument by yourself or with others. For those who don't play an instrument, sing, dance to a beat, or be creative.

<u>Daily Dining</u>
If you are tired after work or had a hard day at home, order out food if you can. Cook something easy at home or ask for help in getting food in.

<u>Daily Reading/Listen to the News</u>
Learning in any form is good. If the news is too dramatic, turn the television or internet off. Read about subjects that are calming.

<u>Daily Pillow and Bed Sleep Sculpting</u>
Turn off your computer hours before you go to bed. Get your pillow and your bed covers ready. Sculptor yourself into bed."

Diary Entry 88 - March 12

Questioning things caused a sobbing awareness of myself. This perception was forming a slinky style circle around me. My worry, I hoped, would soon center itself on me.

Diary Entry 89 - March 15

Oh, what a food lover I was last night. Everything was eaten without an appetite. This hand to mouth action dissolved food, Drano-style, down my throat.

My familiar food routine, stimulus-response behavior, needed to yield to healthier habits.

Diary Entry 90 - March 20

I decided to call Speet.

"Hi Speet," I said.

"Hi Mom. I don't have a ton of time to talk. I'm playing music tonight and need to practice."

"I won't be on long. I wanted to see how you are. How is your music going?" I asked.

"Music is going well. The pay is pretty good and my gigs are consistent. I think I will sign up for one course and see how that goes for the summer," Speet answered.

"That sounds good, Speet. If you do both music and a class, and stress increases, can you remember the Love Dos that we talked about when you were home?" I asked.

"Sure Mom. Let's see, I'm pretty good at Love Do-Daily Rise. I get up within fifteen minutes of my alarm. I almost always grab a protein bar for Breakfast. I try to clean up my place. I shower daily, Love Do-Daily Care of Self. I especially deep breathe for Love Do Daily Deep Breathing and Daily Ping-Pong Communication with a friend or two," Speet answered.

"Sounds great. I know you do the Love Do-Daily Break a Leg Performance with your playing guitar and singing at night. What about your sleeping habits?" I asked.

"I ask for and have been getting the middle set for my music, rather than the late gig. I go on from nine to eleven at night. On the nights that I don't play music, I make a conscious effort to get off the computer a couple of hours before I go to bed," Speet answered.

"Wonderful. It's so nice to hear your voice. I'm so glad I got to talk with you. Love you," I said.

"Love you, too, Mom. Thanks for always caring. I know you worry. I'm trying hard to have a schedule by following the Love Dos. Schedules help me; I taped the Love Dos that you printed out for me on my refrigerator. I see them in the morning when I get something to eat. I even have some in my notes on my phone. Oh, Mom, I need to go and practice," Speet said.

Speet hung up. I knew I talked too much about the Love Dos. I thought it was important for Speet to stick to a routine and do at least some of the Love Dos. I was glad that he taped the Love Dos to the refrigerator and put them in his phone. I hoped they would help him.

Diary Entry 91 - March 24

I fell into a deep sleep. I started dreaming.

I drifted into a bar.

I sat in a bar. I drank a beer, pale like me. I drank with desire, disgust, and despair. I drank with hands of razor thin steel just waiting for someone to nudge me. I laughed at untruthfulness. My dark and light brown cowboy boots kicked the bottom of the bar until the tips of my boots were knuckle white.

I must get a hold of myself. I can't. I circled my head, leading with my chin, to loosen up my stiff neck. I rotated my head, left to right, and shoulder to shoulder. I heard creaky floor noises from my neck that concerned me.

I had an extra oxygen mask on tonight that breathed every other breath for me, giving me a break from life.

I dove off buildings to catch suicide victims, figuratively speaking. Caregivers did that. Deep and dark sides of depression could become seductive voices. We as Caregivers, listened and looked for differences in our loved ones, anything so we could squash those voices of evil.

When someone had symptoms that appeared different because their symptoms didn't seem rational, were disruptive, and/or had poor insight, some people felt a right to say harsh, judgmental words to them. That was one reason I mind killed.

I advocated care in every thought, word, and movement. My thoughts went to a song, playing in the bar. The song sounded majestic. I jumped up, unaware of who was there. I didn't care.

My blood rose in temperature. Moments of mindlessness and wild dancing was the primer of my release night of feelings. I heard and felt every word of every note while dancing. Singing transcended me into the perceived lines of music going around.

My dark, ruler long hair, hardened and stuck straight out. As my head bopped to music, I saw the knife-like strands of my hair slicing everyone in the bar. What a sight.

I left the bar. The door carried my body across the threshold. Crossing that threshold tamed my ruler hair and softened my sharpness enough to walk home.

I looked around as I walked.

As my head moved around, my eyes opened. I realized that I was in my bed looking at Talking Ceiling.

The whole bar incident was a mind kill/nightmare of release from constantly defending my thoughts, words, and actions to others.

Diary Entry 92 - March 29

Literary caterpillars needed to shed their cocoons to fly in a Caregiver's world.

Diary Entry 93 - March 30

Anxiety was mounting. Heightened sensitivity caved me. Anger boiled me. My skin bubbled with anticipation. My insides fell to my toes. I needed a protective mentor.

I had a twisted Eiffel Tower in my heart. I wanted Dr. Tantrum to be the mentor to untwist my heart enough to stand straight, shine, and survive as tall as the real Eiffel Tower.

Diary Entry 94 - April 2

Vigilante rightfulness in thoughts and actions couldn't be judged unless you were the vigilante. Watching loved ones suffer, ached, until justice was felt and served.

Should laws be interrupted and manipulated to prove what you want them to? Don't some judges manipulate their final verdict in terms of their left or rightness? Don't some District Attorneys indict and arrest some and look the other way for others? Shouldn't any verdict/arrest be based on justice, truth, the law, and nothing else?

Disease threw darts and targeted loved ones. Not fair, not right, grounds for vigilante runs. The never-ending adrenaline, the lack of feeling, the focus, the thought-out plans, and seeking justice supported my vigilante mind killings.

I grew up Catholic. Were there any vigilante Saints? I bet there were. I would be judged for my thoughts and actions by God when He wanted me. It was something I had to live with.

Easter was almost here with the popping up of tulips and daffodils. I spent a fair amount of time in church during Easter season in my younger years. The Stations of the Cross, which were said before Easter, wounded me every time we said them.

Suffering was severe for Jesus. Jesus was misunderstood and shunned by many.

The mentally ill suffered, were misunderstood, shunned, and felt alone much of their life.

A similarity flashed by my mind, and I wrote the Stations of the Ill, the old-fashioned way, with paper and a pen.

I told myself that today, Good Friday, I would go to St. Augustine Church and say The Stations of the Cross. I would also say the Stations of the Ill.

I was in Church waiting for the priest to start the Stations of the Cross. I would whisper to myself the Stations of the Ill after the church ones were said.

"Please stand. In the name of the Father, the Son, and the Holy Spirit. The first station of the Cross, Jesus is condemned to death. We adore you, Oh Christ, and we bless you," Father Quinn said.

Genuflecting, I said, "Because by your Holy Cross you redeemed the world."

Prayers were said and then I whispered, "Mental illness is condemned to death."

"The second station of the Cross, Jesus carries his cross. We adore you, Oh Christ, and we bless you," Father Quinn said.

And so, the Stations of the Cross said by Father Quinn and the Stations of the Ill whispered by me, went on in the same fashion until Station 14.

Stations of the Cross and Stations of the Ill:

"Station 1: Jesus is condemned to death. Mental illness is condemned to death.

Station 2: Jesus carries his cross. Many bare tremendous pains.

Station 3: Jesus falls for the first time. Mental illness falls on a loved one for the first time.

Station 4: Jesus meets his Mother. Caregivers/Mothers and loved ones handle the illness together.

Station 5: Simon helps Jesus carry his cross. Caregivers help their loved ones carry their pain.

Station 6: Veronica wipes the face of Jesus. A Caregiver wipes the face of their loved one.

Station 7: Jesus falls for the second time. A relapse of mental illness falls on a loved one for a second time.

Station 8: Women of Jerusalem cry for Jesus. Caregivers weep for their loved ones.

Station 9: Jesus falls for the third time. A relapse of mental illness falls on a loved one for a third time. We must go on with hope.

Station 10: Jesus's clothes are taken away. Doctors, specialists, researchers, and Caregivers strip away the negative power of mental illness.

Station 11: Jesus is nailed to the cross. Medicine and new insights nail down better treatments.

Station 12: Jesus dies on the cross. Mental illness dies.

Station 13: The body of Jesus is taken down from the cross. Stigma is taken down. Doors open to a better life.

Station 14: Jesus is laid in the tomb. Mental illness is cured for all that suffer."

My whispering stopped.

I sat tall in my wooden pew of hope.

Diary Entry 95 - April 5

The first lines of The Serenity Prayer were, "God grant me the serenity to accept the things I cannot change; Courage to change the things I can; And wisdom to know the difference."

"Say The Serenity Prayer," said specialists and well-wishers.

I knew the Prayer helped many and I applauded that. But for me, nothing was typical, nothing was serene or acceptable, nothing made sense.

The next line of the longer version of the Serenity Prayer was, "Living one day at a time, enjoying one moment at a time." That line of the Serenity Prayer spoke to me. I prayed to God to help me do that.

I fought stigma, preached awareness, brawled for understanding of symptoms by all, and advocated for Caregivers' wisdom, experiences, and voices to be heard.

That was my prayer, my courage, and my wisdom for now.

Diary Entry 96 - April 8

Caregiving enhanced a talent into an art of the heart. What joy there was in helping and seeing the smiles of others.

Diary Entry 97 - April 21

I walked outside at five o'clock in the morning. I was alone with a wonderful, unexpected snow. It rained the previous night. The snow fell on all the maple, oak, and pine trees. The boxwood bushes glistened. The freezing rain acted as double-sided tape uniting the branches beneath it and the snow on top of it. The combination of the freezing rain and snow formed sculptures of weeping beauty. This was a gift no one could refuse.

I wore a red down-filled coat that puffed warmth around me. I marveled at the stillness of sound.

My black gloves shook hands with the branches. Snow fell everywhere. The cold snow swirled around me, refreshing everything. As the snow fell off the branches, the branches moved up and breathed a little.

It was beautiful.

Diary Entry 98 - May 9

I found myself not writing as much in *The Diary of a Caregiver*.

My writing bowed to Dr. Tantrum. His office was a new entry in my life.

Diary Entry 99 - May 18

Time flew by. I missed seeing my Lovelies at Concerned Care.

Bessie and I got on the road. There was little traffic. We arrived in record time.

"Good morning, Crystal. Last time I was here, I missed seeing you. How are you?" I asked.

"I'm fine. I am working hard in my courses and coming here as much as I can. I need the money and I enjoy seeing everyone," Crystal answered.

"I'm eager to see my Lovelies. I will see you on the way out," I said.

"Okay, Mrs. Patstegre. Say hi to Mr. Gaudan for me. He broke out of his shell. He is a different person. Everyone enjoys talking with him now," Crystal said.

"I will tell Mr. Gaudan that you say hi," I said.

I was glad Crystal was getting to know some of the lovely people at Concerned Care. They needed companionship. Being alone was sometimes their only choice.

"There you are my gray cart. Did you miss me? We have a job to do this morning. Do you have cobwebs on you? Let me look. No, you don't," I said out loud.

I arranged everything on the cart.

Today I brought small little vases which I filled with water. I lined them up on my cart. I clipped daffodils, trumpets of yellow and orange, from my backyard. I put two daffodils in each vase.

"We're ready to roll, gray cart of kindness. I just need to put the medically approved snacks on your second shelf and off we go," I said.

I proceeded to visit my Lovelies. I wanted to ask Ms. File about Gus from the soup kitchen when I saw her.

I went into the rooms. Most seemed to cheer up with conversation, coupled with the daffodils and other goodies they wanted.

I knocked on Ms. File's door. She had a wreath with spring flowers hanging on her door. That was a new addition to the hallway.

"Come in," said Ms. File.

"Hi, Ms. File. It is Mrs. Patstegre."

"Oh, Mrs. Patstegre, it is so nice to see you. I enjoy it when you visit," Ms. File said.

"Thank you, Ms. File. I enjoy seeing you, too. How have you been? Have you seen Mr. Gaudan?" I asked.

"I have seen Mr. Gaudan every day. I am so glad you introduced us. Would you mind if we walk down to his room? We can all talk together," Ms. File answered.

"Sure, Ms. File. Before we go, I was wondering if you can answer a question for me. It concerns one of your former students, Gus. He works with me at Hookum Soup Kitchen for the homeless. He told me he was finishing college courses and was getting extra credit by volunteering at Hookum. I sensed that his reasons for being at Hookum were not what they appeared to be," I said.

"Well, Mrs. Patstegre, after you were here last, I found out that Gus is an undercover detective for the Ladin Police Department, where the homeless community and Hookum are located. I was right when I told you before that I thought he was involved with the law in some way.

"He is finishing up his college degree, even though he is a little older than most. He is volunteering at Hookum to catch drug dealers who have been harming, promoting drugs, and stealing from the homeless," Ms. File said.

"Thank you, Ms. File for trusting me. I won't tell anyone," I said.

I was relieved. It was Gus's nature to be inquisitive being a police detective. It was my nature to be suspicious after what happened to Speet.

"Ms. File, can we walk to Mr. Gaudan's room now?" I asked.

"Yes, let's go," Ms. File answered.

We walked to Mr. Gaudan's room. Her pace seemed fast to me considering Ms. File's age.

Ms. File knocked on the door. Mr. Gaudan answered.

"Good morning. My two favorite girls are here to see me. Come on in. Sit down," Mr. Gaudan said.

"Mr. Gaudan, your hair is combed. You beam with joy. I love the good mood air that follows you. I brought a few daffodils for you for spring cheer. Would you like your usual *Wall Street Journal*? Would you like a snack today?" I asked.

"I will take both. Thank you for the beautiful daffodils," Mr. Gaudan answered.

Ms. File and I sat down. Ms. File and Mr. Gaudan gazed at each other. Eagerness on their tongues seemed to be their breakfast this morning.

Ms. File scooted up on her chair.

"Mrs. Patstegre, Mr. Gaudan and I are getting married. I want to experience marriage with this fine man. God wanted us to meet. We love each other. We will move into larger accommodations here. The wedding will take place soon. We will let you know the day when we know. Do you think you can come, Mrs. Patstegre?" Ms. File asked.

"I would not miss your special day. I'm excited and happy for both of you," I answered.

Who would have thought so much love would evolve between beautiful Ms. File and gruff Mr. Gaudan. Ms. File, the beauty, tamed Mr. Gaudan with her love. He became her prince. I am happy and sappy. A tear was enjoying itself on my check and then another tear came. Cinderella was my favorite fairytale growing up. It still was.

I blew two kisses toward my two Lovelies on my way out.

"Oh, I forgot, Ms. File. Who said, 'When we do the best we can, we never know what miracle is wrought in our life, or in the life of another?'" I asked.

"That's easy, Mrs. Patstegre. It was Helen Keller, someone I admire. Good choice for a quote," Ms. File answered.

Ms. File blew me a kiss as I headed out.

I drove home. I shared the news with Talking Ceiling that Ms. File and Mr. Gaudan were getting married.

Talking Ceiling and I were very happy.

Diary Entry 100 - June 15

"Talking Ceiling, I want to thank you for talking with me when I needed you. Thank you for listening," I said.

"I'm always here for you," Talking Ceiling said.

"Speet and I talk routinely whenever one or the other has something to say. He is happy from what I can tell. He plays his music at night. He's deciding if taking a course at campus during the summer will work with his music schedule," I said.

"I stretch with delight for you, Mrs. Patstegre. Knowing Speet is happy is a good thing," Talking Ceiling said.

"Yes, Talking Ceiling, it is a good thing. It gets lonely without Speet here. Many thanks for stomping out that loneliness," I said.

"Now, Mrs. Patstegre, yawn yourself to sleep. I'll watch over you," said Talking Ceiling.

Many nights Talking Ceiling stretched out her arms. I never knew that until recently. When Talking Ceiling thought I was asleep, I saw her hands descend to me. I assumed she did that every night.

Tonight, when I fell asleep, I got a nice surprise. As with previous nights, I heard faint guitar and mandolin music playing in the background.

"I don't think you need my arms tonight. Your breathing is silent and your movements still. I'm available for you if you wake up. Good night, Mrs. Patstegre, Caregiver to many, love of my life," Talking Ceiling said.

Did I hear love of my life from Talking Ceiling's mouth? Was I dreaming? I didn't think so. Tonight, just this one time, Mr. Patstegre, love of my life, acknowledged his presence. Was he trying to tell me that he had always been with me? I wondered how many times he looked over me while I slept. Maybe every night. Maybe I haven't ever been alone.

Diary Entry 101 – July 1

Today I enrolled in a virtual class about police reform. I periodically took classes on police reform ever since Speet's unfortunate incident with law enforcement.

I watched a tall, thin, young, scared, confused, and anxious man acting out because of his fear and anxiety. Suddenly, four large officers appeared, held him down, handcuffed him, shackled him, and choke-held him. Shortly thereafter, the young man stopped moving.

The teacher explained that the young man died a little later from his harsh treatment of being misunderstood.

I moved a little on my desk chair. I stood up. I gasped for air. My heart pounded so hard I felt dizzy. The physical attack on that young man, without me realizing it, triggered me. What I saw in this virtual classroom churned up buried emotions from past traumas I went through with Speet.

I was not scared. I was unfinished.

I got off my computer and left the class. I took deep breaths. I got out the cuff of reality and pumped it around my arm. God, it got tight. The cuff popped off; the danger lights blinked and reality hit. Buried emotions caused awful physical symptoms.

I possessed no coping skills for unresolved feelings.

The ability to stay focused on the task at hand as a Caregiver relied on the imaginary, numbing, morphine IV drip given in my creative, made-up recovery room. This IV-ID defied the stages of grief, defined me, became my planner, my life, and my legs, while I cared for others. I was confused.

Was this a warning from the Almighty? If I didn't give up my safe recovery room existence, would I see God earlier than I wanted?

I needed help. I needed care. I wanted help. I wanted care.

I called Dr. Tantrum.

"I need help, Dr. Tantrum. I need to talk, get answers. Can you squeeze me in today?" I asked.

"I took the afternoon off from seeing clients to work on other things in my office. I can take a break from what I am working on. You can come over now," Dr. Tantrum answered.

"I am on my way. Thank you," I said.

Bessie and I sped to Dr. Tantrum's office.

I sat in his waiting room. As I waited, I heard everything and everyone. My focused Caregiving life prevented me from seeing many things. Until now. My unrest, unwilling to calm itself, was threatening me. I must deal with it.

I was aware of something different that was disturbing and at the same time, distinguished. I was aware of something that wanted more for me than I did. That something wanted me to smell, see, hear, touch, and taste everything every day, not just with the rain and snow.

I believed twisted and tornado like thoughts could be funneled into understanding conversations and explanations.

I believed Dr. Tantrum to be an archeological find.

Dr. Tantrum's door opened. He walked toward me. I walked toward him.

"Good afternoon. Come on in, Mrs. Patstegre," Dr. Tantrum said.

"Good afternoon, Dr. Tantrum. Thanks for seeing me," I said.

He looked a little swollen and dark under his eyes. Helping others live a happier existence was tiring, I thought, from one racoon to another.

I sat down, looked around, questioned everything, and wondered if he could handle a Caregiver like me. Sometimes, I offered him little or no help. Would he see me picking up his codes of behavior? Would he pick up mine? Would he connect the dots of my diary without knowing of its existence?

"Let's sit for a while without talking," he said.

I broke the stillness.

"I took a virtual class on police reform today. They showed a video of a young man, who looked like my son. He was confined, handcuffed, and was acting out from perceived symptoms of mental illness and confusion. Using old tactics to constrain this young man, he died from lack of oxygen. The class showed this video to show that these old hold tactics should not and were not being done today," I said.

"I'm sorry you saw that," Dr Tantrum said.

"It was especially disturbing because Speet, my son, experienced a similar situation many years ago. Within minutes of watching this video, my heart sped up. I was dizzy, nauseous, and scared.

"Exposure to the video in my class bypassed my anger and touched the buried true sadness in me. The sadness triggered me to the past and centipeded in all directions. It spiked my blood pressure, panic attacked me, and gave unexpected perceived death threats. Would hard core feelings kill me?" I asked.

"No, Mrs. Patstegre hard core emotions will not kill you. I will counsel you at your pace and willingness to learn skills to diminish physical symptoms when you experience fear when triggered. Together we will explore what is best for you," Dr. Tantrum answered.

"I need to stay alive to care for Speet. My high blood pressure made me realize that caring for myself would benefit everyone," I said.

"Mrs. Patstegre, I listen to you. I will lead you down a path using my academia knowledge. I will fine tune my knowledge to your situation. Your experience, knowledge, and intuitive wisdom, helps me understand you," Dr. Tantrum said.

Dr. Tantrum's brain rubberbanded his tongue from saying the "feeling" word too much. He commented on my physical symptoms. He was a smart man.

I knew my insides needed spectacles with a strong prescription to really see again. Dr. Tantrum might write that prescription someday. He might be the prescription.

"My body and my mind started screaming at me. Submerged and subconscious feelings numbered together and fired off missile voices. I finally heard them after many, many years. The screams of reality were competing with my fear of collapsing," I said.

"I can help with those screams. Whenever and whatever you release to me, I will dissect, validate, answer your questions, whatever helps you the most. Your years of Caregiving should be noticed and given importance. I believe that your knowledge and experience from Caregiving and my knowledge when entwined, will enhance the outcome you are searching for," said Dr. Tantrum.

I hoped Dr. Tantrum could make a fraction of what he said come true.

Could I help Dr. Tantrum help me? Yes. I needed and finally wanted to leave the fear-farm and shovel out the manure.

"Who will I be if I venture out? Can I trust that you can assist such a transition? Can I balance decreasing anger and increasing sadness to aid the recovery process and still stay focused on the task at hand?" I asked.

"Yes, you can, Mrs. Patstegre," Dr. Tantrum answered.

I grinned.

"I can help you. This is what I do, Mrs. Patstegre. I assure you my intuition will be on high alert," Dr. Tantrum said.

"I believe you can help me," I said.

"Wanting to take care of yourself is reaching out to you," Dr. Tantrum said.

I took a deep breath. He was right.

ACKNOWLEDGMENTS

I remember Mary Jane and Arthur Powell as loving parents, as aging and wise Lovelies, and as angels in heaven.

I am most grateful to my loving husband, Mark Daly. His amazing skill from writing two business books provided outstanding edits, publishing/layout knowledge, and invaluable help with the cover of the book. Even though *The Diary of a Caregiver* is fictional, Mark used his creative thinking to critique, while understanding that maintaining my voice was essential to the feel of the book.

I am very grateful to Gregg Daly, my son, for his ideas, feedback, help with the back cover of the book, and brilliant guidance concerning plot, theme, and character development. He has generated remarkable screenplays and teleplays with his penetrating imagination and wisdom.

Patrick Daly, my son, gave words of inspiration throughout my writing journey. His motivating remarks to me were sparked from his creative ability to unite and ignite his emotions and words into many unique original songs.

Erin Powell, my sister, was most generous with her time. She thoroughly read the draft several times. Her detailed line editing and sharp eyes caught grammar mistakes. She was very beneficial.

A great deal of thanks go out to my dear friend, Karen Rahn. She constantly cheered me on. Her refreshing choice of words made me laugh and lit up my mind with ideas.

Although not directly involved in the editing process, I would like to recognize another son, Steven Daly, my sister-in-law, Caryl Daly and two other siblings, Tish Bright and Arthur Powell for their support.

ABOUT THE AUTHOR

Gigi Daly, a summa cum laude graduate in psychology, has used her strong insight her entire life. She is LEAP...Listen-Empathize-Agree-Partner certified, a program created by Dr. Amador, and is a volunteer speaker with NAMI...National Alliance on Mental Illness.

Family and friends, so important to her, have been recipients of her heart felt poems and writings. Her love for writing free flowing feelings, enticed her words to flyover into a debut novel, *The Diary of a Caregiver*. Her accumulation of words grew into a field of stories and diary entries with captivating meaning.

When not writing, she can be seen helping run two businesses with her husband, teaching her grandson, Markus, piano, grabbing, as she says, "the right shot at the right moment" with her photography, applauding loved ones' achievements, making birthdays, holidays, and celebrations memorable, and seeking to improve the lives of others through Caregiving.

www.ingramcontent.com/pod-product-compliance
Lightning Source LLC
Chambersburg PA
CBHW071836020726
47502CB00004B/1380